BODYGUARD

Book 1: Recruit

Also by Chris Bradford

The Bodyguard Series
Book 1: Recruit
Book 2: Hostage
Book 3: Hijack
Book 4: Ransom

Book 1: Recruit

Chris Bradford

Philomel Books

PHILOMEL BOOKS
an imprint of Penguin Random House LLC
375 Hudson Street
New York, NY 10014

Philomel Books is a registered trademark of Penguin Random House LLC.

Library of Congress Cataloging-in-Publication Data is available upon request.
Printed in the United States of America.
ISBN 9781524736972
10 9 8 7 6 5 4 3 2 1

American edition edited by Brian Geffen.
American edition design by Jennifer Chung.
Text set in 11-point Palatino Nova.
This is a work of fiction. Names, characters, places, and incidents either are the
product of the author's imagination or are used fictitiously, and any resemblance
to actual persons, living or dead, businesses, companies, events, or locales is
entirely coincidental.

For Zach and Leo.

May you protect each other through life . . .

"The best bodyguard is the one nobody notices."

With the rise of teen stars, the intense media focus on celebrity families and a new wave of millionaires and billionaires, adults are no longer the only target for hostage-taking, blackmail and assassination— kids are too.

That's why they need specialized protection ...

GUARDIAN

Guardian is a secret close-protection organization that differs from all other security outfits by training and supplying only young bodyguards.

Known as guardians, these highly skilled kids are more effective than the typical adult bodyguard, who can easily draw unwanted attention. Operating invisibly as a child's constant companion, a guardian provides the greatest possible protection for any high-profile or vulnerable young target.

In a life-threatening situation, a **guardian** is the final ring of defense.

PROLOGUE

The driver's knuckles turned white as he gripped the steering wheel of the Humvee and planted his foot hard on the pedal. The immense engine roared, and the armored vehicle shot onto the bomb-blasted road.

As the Humvee tore across the potholed concrete that stretched into the distance like the cracked skin of a dead snake, the two passengers in the back could only stare at the hellish images of a war-torn Iraq whipping past their windows: barren patches of garbage-strewn desert, burned-out carcasses of abandoned vehicles, crumbling buildings pockmarked with bullet holes, and the haunted faces of Iraqi children scavenging among the rubble.

The younger of the two passengers, a fresh-faced female diplomatic aide with styled blond hair, wiped away a tear with an unsteady hand. The other, a tall, handsome Hispanic man with strong cheekbones and deep brown eyes as sharp as an eagle's, was more composed. Yet his tense grip on the seat's armrest betrayed his deeper unease.

The bodyguard alone remained impassive, strapped into the front passenger seat, his MP5 submachine gun across his lap. He'd survived this run many times. Not that it made the drive any easier. Less than eight miles long, this sweeping bend of road was the sole artery that connected Baghdad International Airport to the Green Zone—the fortress-like military and governmental safe haven in the heart of Baghdad. This made Route Irish the most dangerous stretch of highway in the world—a ready-made shooting gallery for terrorists and insurgents. Any attempt to travel the route was little more than a suicidal dash.

And today the stakes are even higher, thought the bodyguard, glancing over his shoulder at the newly appointed US ambassador to Iraq. Usually the Americans arranged for a helicopter to transport senior officials between the airport and the zone, but high winds and the threat of a sandstorm had grounded all aircraft.

The bodyguard's eyes scanned the terrain beyond the bulletproof glass. In front and behind were three more Humvees thundering down the highway, forming a formidable military escort. These vehicles were armed to the teeth with mounted M2 heavy machine guns and MK19 grenade launchers. As the convoy raced along, the lead Humvee cleared the road ahead, knocking civilian vehicles to one side if they didn't move out of the way quickly enough.

An underpass came into view, and the bodyguard tensed. This was a prime spot for an attack. The bridge would have been swept for improvised explosive devices the night before. But that didn't mean *all* the IEDs had been discovered. His hand instinctively felt for the key fob in his pocket. He carried it with him everywhere. It contained a photo of his smiling eight-year-old son. Squeezing the talisman, the bodyguard vowed—as he always did—to survive the journey, if only for the sake of his son.

As they passed beneath the graffiti-scrawled bridge, he kept his eyes peeled for "dickers"—lookouts who phoned ahead to rebel fighters lying in wait. The call might trigger a vehicle packed with explosives, a roadside IED, a suicide bomber, a drive-by shooting or even a barrage of mortars and rocket-propelled grenades. The bodyguard had witnessed all these assaults at one time or another, and they always ended in tragedy.

Emerging on the other side of the underpass, he heard the driver breathe a sigh of relief as he gunned the Humvee faster toward the Green Zone. The bodyguard resumed his surveillance sweep—scouring for threats among the surrounding traffic, the tree stumps on the central reservation, the housing estates to the south, and the approaching overpass and ramps of the next concrete-jungle intersection.

"This isn't good," muttered the driver as their convoy began to slow to a snail's pace. In the distance the traffic had ground to a halt.

The HF radio burst into life. *"Tango One to Tango Three. Collision up ahead."*

From the rear vehicle, the team leader responded, *"Tango One, this is Tango Three. Push on through. Use the central reservation."*

The lead vehicle approached the holdup. As it mounted the curb, the bodyguard's attention was drawn to a dead dog lying at the side of the road. The carcass, left to rot in the sun, appeared unnaturally bloated.

Then, as their own vehicle drew closer, the bodyguard spotted a man on the overpass, talking into his phone. The bodyguard's instincts kicked into overdrive, and he reached across to yank the steering wheel hard right. Startled, the driver gave him a furious look as their Humvee veered off the highway.

A split second later the booby-trapped dog exploded, engulfing the lead vehicle in a ball of flame.

The blast rocked their own Humvee with its intensity. The aide screamed in terror as a wave of hellfire rolled toward them. Keeping his composure, the bodyguard scanned the horizon and, out of the corner of his eye, spotted the telltale flare of a rocket-propelled grenade being fired from a nearby block of flats.

"GO, GO, GO!" he bawled at the driver.

The soldier floored the accelerator, and the engine

screamed in protest. They shot forward, but it was too late. The RPG struck their rear end and detonated. Despite the Humvee weighing more than two and a half tons, the vehicle flipped into the air like a child's toy. Inside, the occupants were thrown around like rag dolls. The Humvee landed with a tremendous crash upon the driver's side. Instantly the cabin filled with smoke and the acrid stench of burning paint and diesel.

The bodyguard's ears rang as he fought to orient himself. Wedging himself in his seat, he looked around to check on his Principal, the likely target of the attack. The Humvee had been up-armored to withstand such attacks, but a direct hit meant the damage was still devastating. The bodyguard also knew a second strike would be the end for them.

"Sir? SIR!" he shouted, waving away the smoke to find the ambassador. "Are you okay?"

Dazed but conscious, the ambassador nodded.

"We have to get out *now!*" the bodyguard explained, reaching back and undoing the man's seat belt. He tapped the driver on the shoulder. "You take the second Principal."

But the driver didn't respond. He was dead, his head having smashed against the windshield.

Cursing, the bodyguard tried to push open the front passenger door. But even with his full body weight against it, he couldn't budge it. The force of the explosion had twisted the Humvee's heavily armored construction, and the door was jammed shut. They were trapped like sardines in a can.

Grabbing his gun from the footwell, he now prayed the bulletproof glass was one-way, as he'd requested.

"Cover your face!" the bodyguard ordered the ambassador.

Aiming the MP5 at the far corner of the windshield, the bodyguard fired off several rounds and the glass exploded outward. He kicked the screen free, the smoke cleared and he crawled through the opening.

Outside, a full-on firefight was occurring. Earsplitting blasts of grenades and the thunder of heavy machine guns mixed with the concussive explosion of mortars. The air was thick with black smoke and the *whizz* of speeding bullets.

Turning back, he helped the ambassador clamber from the Humvee and pulled him into the cover of its chassis.

"Hayley!" the ambassador implored, looking at his aide hanging limp in the backseat.

But the bodyguard had already clocked her condition. The young woman had taken the full force of the RPG. He shook his head regretfully. "She's dead."

Sheltering the ambassador from gunfire, he signaled for the backup team. The rear Humvee driver spotted them and steered in their direction as a white sedan came tearing down the road from behind. Before any evasive action was possible, the rogue car was alongside. A second later it exploded. The Humvee was annihilated in the blast, taking with it the entire crew and any hope of rescue.

The bodyguard needed no further proof that this had been a carefully coordinated attack. A simultaneous assault of IEDs, RPGs and suicide bombers meant the rebels had known the ambassador's itinerary and were going all out to assassinate him.

With the operation so jeopardized, the bodyguard decided he had to break protocol if he was to save his Principal's life. Besides, it was only a matter of time before another rocket hit their disabled Humvee.

"We're sitting ducks out here," said the bodyguard. "Are you able to run?"

"Won the four-hundred-meter dash at UCLA," replied the ambassador.

"Then stay close and do exactly as I say. We're heading for the underpass."

He let loose a spray of covering fire. Then, using his body as a shield, he grabbed the ambassador and led him across open ground. As they dashed for safety, the supersonic crack of rebel bullets flew past their heads.

Behind them, an RPG hit their Humvee. The two of them were thrown to the ground by the explosion. Adrenaline pumped to the max, the bodyguard dragged the ambassador back to his feet.

Diving for cover behind a battered BMW, he stopped to assess their situation. The last surviving Humvee was battling to suppress enemy fire. The few Iraqi civilians who hadn't reached the underpass cowered behind their cars. The bodyguard knew most would be innocent civilians, but he kept his gun primed: it would take only one rebel to kill the ambassador.

Peering around the hood, he sighted a black SUV with tinted windows rolling down a nearby on-ramp. Its passenger window was open, a gun barrel poking out in their direction.

Suddenly the BMW erupted with the pepper of bullets, and its windshield shattered. The bodyguard dropped on top of the ambassador, shielding him from the deadly shots. The car took the worst of the assault as round after round rattled its bodywork. Then the barrage ceased as the surviving Humvee's machine-gunner turned his sights on the rebels' SUV, forcing them to change target.

"We can't get pinned down here," the bodyguard grunted, rolling off the ambassador.

Staying low, they weaved between the cars toward the underpass, a hail of bullets following close on their tails. As soon as they were beneath its shelter, the bodyguard hunted for a car that wasn't blocked in by the obviously prearranged accident. He spotted a silver Mercedes-Benz near the front of the pileup.

The blast of a machine gun and terrified screams echoed through the underpass.

"They're following us!" exclaimed the ambassador, glancing over his shoulder in alarm.

Pushing his Principal ahead, the bodyguard returned fire, ensuring he was between the ambassador and the gunmen at all times.

Zigzagging through the cars, they were almost at the Mercedes when the ambassador came to a dead stop.

"Keep going!" urged the bodyguard.

Then he too saw the man standing before them.

Dressed in jeans and T-shirt, his face hidden behind a red-and-white headscarf, the rebel held an AK-47 assault rifle aimed directly at the ambassador.

He fired.

Instinctively the bodyguard leaped in front of the ambassador, knocking him aside. The ambassador could only watch as his savior was thrown back by the blaze of bullets, then crashed to the floor—lifeless.

The bodyguard had made the ultimate sacrifice to save him.

But it would all be in vain. The rebel strode over and planted the smoking barrel of the AK-47 in the ambassador's face.

"Now *you* die, infidel!" snarled the rebel.

"You can murder me, but you won't murder hope," said the ambassador, staring defiantly back at the insurgent.

By all rights, the bodyguard should have been killed instantly, but his bulletproof vest had protected him from the worst of the assault. He was barely conscious, and only his deeply ingrained training allowed him to react. He'd lost hold of his MP5, but he pulled a SIG Sauer P228 from his hip and shot the rebel at point-blank range.

Before the man had even hit the ground, the bodyguard was struggling to his feet. His limbs felt as heavy as lead, and there was a worrying coppery taste in his mouth.

"You're alive!" exclaimed the ambassador, rushing to his aid.

Staggering over to the Mercedes, the bodyguard yanked the door open. The driver had already fled for his life, leaving the keys in the ignition.

"Get in and stay low," he instructed the ambassador, gasping for breath.

Fumbling with the keys, he begged the car to start as the back window imploded from a strafing of bullets. The engine kicked into life, the bodyguard slammed his foot on the accelerator and they shot out onto Route Irish. A hail of gunfire rained down on them from the bridge above. Weaving to avoid it, the bodyguard powered down the road, swerving around potholes, until the thunder of battle receded into the distance.

"You're seriously hurt!" said the ambassador, noticing the driver's seat was dripping with blood.

The bodyguard barely acknowledged him as he focused the last of his strength on carrying out his duty. Approaching the blast-walled safety of the Green Zone's first checkpoint, he slowed the Mercedes. The sentries would have no idea he was carrying the ambassador and would more than likely shoot first. Stopping short of the barrier, he got out of the car with the ambassador and walked the final stretch.

Still scanning for threats, the bodyguard stumbled, blood now soaking through his combats.

"We must get you to a hospital," the ambassador insisted, taking his arm.

The bodyguard looked absently down at himself. Only now with the adrenaline fading did the pain register. "Too late for that," he said, grimacing.

United Nations soldiers rushed out, surrounding them in a protective cordon.

"You're safe now, sir," said the bodyguard as he collapsed at the ambassador's feet, a small bloodstained key fob clutched in his hand.

1

Six years later . . .

The fist caught Connor by surprise. A rocketing right hook that jarred his jaw. Stars burst before his eyes, and he stumbled backward. Only instinct saved him from getting floored by the left cross that followed. Blocking the punch with his forearm, Connor countered with a kick to the ribs. But he was too dazed to deliver any real power.

His attacker, a boy with knotted black hair and a body that seemed to have been chiseled from stone, deflected the strike and charged at him in a thunderous rage. Connor shielded his head as a barrage of blows rained down on him.

"GO, JET! KNOCK 'IM OUT!"

The shouts of the crowd were a monstrous roar in Connor's ears as Jet pummeled him. Connor ducked and weaved to escape the brutal onslaught. But he was boxed in.

Then the ding of the bell cut through the clamor and the referee stepped between them. Jet glared at Connor, his advantage lost.

Connor returned to his corner. He sported spiky brown hair, green-blue eyes and an athletic physique—the benefit of several years of martial arts training. Spitting out his mouth guard, he gratefully accepted the water bottle Dan held out for him. His kickboxing instructor, bald-headed with narrow eyes and a flattened nose that had been broken one too many times, didn't look happy.

"You have to keep your guard up," Dan warned.

"Jet's so quick with his hands," gasped Connor between gulps of water.

"But you're quicker," Dan replied, his tone firm and unquestionable. "The championship title is yours for the taking. *Unless* you persist in exposing your chin like that."

Connor nodded. Summoning up his last reserves of energy, he stretched his arms and breathed deeply, trying to shake the stiffness from his burning muscles. After competing in six qualifying bouts, he was tired. But he'd trained hard for the Battle of Britain tournament and wasn't going to fall at the last hurdle.

Dan wiped the sweat off Connor's face with a towel. "See the guy in the second row?"

Connor glanced toward a man in his late forties with silver-gray hair trimmed into a severe crew cut. He sat among the cheering spectators, a tournament program in one hand, his eyes discreetly studying Connor.

"He's a manager scouting for talent."

All of a sudden Connor felt an additional pressure to succeed. This could be his chance at the international circuit, to compete for world titles and even earn sponsorship deals. Besides his own ambition, he knew his family could really use the money.

The bell rang for the third and final round.

"Now go win this fight!" Dan urged, giving Connor an encouraging slap on the back.

Popping the mouth guard into his mouth, Connor stood to face Jet—determined to win more than ever.

His opponent bobbed lightly on his toes, seemingly as fresh as in the first round. The crowd whooped and hollered as the two fighters squared up beneath the white-hot glare of the ring's spotlights. They stared at each other, neither willing to show the slightest sign of weakness. As soon as their gloves touched, Jet launched straight into his attack—a blistering combination of jab, cross, jab, hook.

Connor evaded the punches and countered with a front kick. The ball of his foot collided with Jet's stomach, and his opponent doubled over. Keeping up the pressure, Connor trapped Jet against the ropes with a torrent of punches. But Jet refused to back down. With the ferocity of a cornered tiger, he blasted Connor with multiple body blows. Each strike weakened Connor a little more, and he was forced to retreat. As he stepped away, Jet caught him with a crippling shin kick to the thigh. Connor buckled, opening himself up to another hook punch. Jet threw all his weight behind the attack. At the last second, Connor ducked, and the fist glanced off the top of his head.

Realizing he'd been lucky to escape the hook this time, Connor now knew Jet was gunning to knock him down with *that* punch.

Like two gladiators, they battled back and forth across the ring. Sweat poured from Connor's brow, his breathing hard, his blood pumping as the punches and kicks came thick and fast. Connor felt his energy ebbing. But he couldn't give up now. There was too much at stake.

"Stay light on your feet!" bawled Dan from his ringside corner.

Jet launched a roundhouse to the head. Connor double-blocked it with his arms and countered with a side kick. Jet leaped away, then immediately drove back in, fists flying. The crowd now going wild at the epic to-and-fro of combat. Connor's name was chanted to the rafters by his friends from the Tiger Martial Arts Dojo: "CON-NOR! CON-NOR!"

Jet's supporters screamed back with equal ferocity. The shouts reached fever pitch as they entered the closing seconds of the bout. Connor realized that if he didn't knock Jet down, his opponent would likely win on points. But exhaustion was getting the better of him.

"Don't drop your guard!" Dan screamed at him in frustration from his corner.

Jet spotted the gap in Connor's defense and went for it. Jab, cross . . . *hook!*

But Connor had been feigning the weakness to draw his opponent in . . . and Jet had taken the bait. With lightning speed, he sidestepped the attack and thrust in a jab, stunning his opponent. Then, whipping his rear leg around, he executed a spinning hook kick. Jet never saw what hit him as Connor's heel connected with the side of his head. Jet's black mouth guard shot out of his mouth, and he crashed to the deck in a heap. A second later the bell rang to end the fight.

A dazed Jet staggered to his feet, helped by the referee. Connor bowed his respect to his opponent, who gave a begrudging nod in return. The presiding judge stepped into the ring. Clasping a microphone, he announced: "The UK title for the Battle of Britain Junior Kickboxing Tournament goes to . . . CONNOR REEVES!"

The crowd roared in celebration as Connor was presented with the trophy, a silver figure of a kickboxer atop a column of white marble. Connor felt a wave of elation and raised the prize high above his head in acknowledgment of his supporters.

Dan gripped him around the shoulders. "Congratulations, champ!" he said, grinning. "Your father would be so proud of you."

Connor looked up at the glittering trophy and at the cheering spectators. He dearly wished his dad could have been by his side to share this moment. His father was the one who'd encouraged him to start martial arts in the first place. It had been his passion—and it was Connor's too.

"I have to admit, you had me worried there for a second," said Dan.

"Feign and fight," replied Connor. "You taught me that trick, remember? So you deserve to hold this as much as me."

Passing Dan the trophy, he glanced toward the second row and was disappointed to see the silver-haired man had gone.

"Wasn't the manager impressed, then?"

"Oh, I wouldn't worry about him," Dan admitted with a playful wink as he brandished the trophy. "I've no idea who that man was. I just wanted you to fight at the top of your game—and you did!"

2

A chill wind hit Connor as he emerged from the ExCel Center in the London Docklands and headed for the bus stop on Freemasons Road. The gray February sky was unforgiving, the tail end of winter refusing to loosen its grip. But not even the dismal weather could dampen Connor's spirits. He was the UK Kickboxing Champion and had the trophy in his duffel bag to prove it. He couldn't wait to show his gran—she was his biggest fan, after all.

Pulling up the hood of his sweatshirt, Connor shouldered his duffel bag and crossed the bridge spanning the Docklands Light Railway. He dodged the traffic on the opposite side and was passing a row of boarded-up shops when he heard a cry for help.

Halfway down a littered alley, he spotted a well-dressed Indian boy surrounded by a gang of youths. It was obvious that a man heading for the train station had also heard the cry. But, averting his gaze, the man hurried past the scene.

Scared of being knifed, thought Connor. *And who'd blame him?*

But Connor couldn't walk away. *The strong have a duty to protect the weak,* his father had taught him. That was the reason his father had joined the army. And why he'd encouraged Connor to take up martial arts. He never wanted his son to be a victim.

The gang leader shoved the boy against the alley wall and began to rifle through his pockets.

"Leave him alone!" shouted Connor.

Almost as one, the gang turned to face their challenger.

"This ain't got nothing to do with you, mate," said the leader. "Leg it!"

Connor ignored the warning and strode toward them. "He's a friend of mine."

"This loser ain't got no friends," the boy said, spitting at his victim's feet, clearly not believing Connor's bluff.

Drawing level with the gang, Connor eyeballed the leader. Dressed in baggy jeans and a Drake T-shirt, the lad was a good few inches taller than him and well built. With a broad chest, bulging biceps and fists like hammers, the boy regarded Connor as though Connor were a nail waiting to be pounded.

The rest of the gang—two boys and a girl—were less intimidating but still dangerous as a pack. One boy in Converse sneakers, baggy jeans and a gray hoodie held a skateboard, his face pockmarked with pimples. The other wore carbon-copy baggy jeans, a puffer jacket and a red Nike baseball hat, tipped at a "too cool for you" angle on his bleached-blond hair. The girl, who looked to be of Asian origin with a jet-black bob and a piercing through her nose, wore dark eyeshadow, emo-style, and Dr. Martens boots. She shot Connor a hard stare.

"Let's go," said Connor to his new friend, keeping his voice low and even. He didn't want to show how nervous he really was. He might be trained in kickboxing and jujitsu, but he wasn't looking for a fight. His jujitsu teacher had drilled into him that violence was the last resort. Especially when outnumbered four to one—*that* was just asking for trouble.

The boy took a hesitant step toward him, but the gang leader planted a hand on his chest. "You're going nowhere."

Frozen to the spot with fear, the boy looked to Connor in wide-eyed desperation.

A tense standoff now ensued between Connor and the gang. Connor's eyes flicked to each gang member, his duffel bag at the ready to protect himself in case one of them pulled a knife.

"I said, leave him alone," he repeated, edging between the gang and their victim.

"And I said, mind your own business," replied the leader, launching a fist straight at the boy's face.

As the terrified boy let out a yelp, Connor moved in and

deflected the punch with a forearm block. Then he took up a fighting stance, fists raised, defying the gang to come any closer.

Glaring at Connor, the leader broke into a mocking laugh. "Watch out, everyone! It's the Karate Kid!"

Don't laugh too soon, thought Connor, unshouldering his duffel bag.

The leader sized up Connor. Then he swung a wild right hook at Connor's head. With lightning reflexes, Connor ducked, drove forward and delivered a powerful punch to the gut in return.

The unexpected strike should have floored the gang leader, but he was much stronger than he looked. Instead of collapsing, he merely grunted and came back at Connor with a combination of jab, cross and uppercut. Connor went on the defensive. As he blocked each attack, it became blindingly obvious that the leader was a trained boxer. Having underestimated his opponent, Connor rapidly reassessed his tactics. Although Connor was faster, the gang leader had the advantage of power and reach. And, without gloves, this fight had the potential to be deadly—just one of those sledgehammer fists could land him in the hospital.

The bigger they are, the harder they fall, thought Connor, recalling how in jujitsu a larger opponent could be defeated by using their strength against themselves.

As the gang leader let loose a vicious roundhouse punch

to his head, Connor entered inside its arc and spun his body into his attacker. Redirecting the force of the strike, he flung the boy over his hip and body-dropped him to the concrete. The leader hit the ground so hard, all the breath was knocked out of him. The gang stared in disbelief at their fallen leader, while the well-dressed boy could barely suppress a grin of delight at seeing his tormentor squirm in the dirt.

"Get . . . him!" the leader wheezed, unable to rise.

The boy with the Nike baseball hat charged in, executing a flying side kick. Connor leaped to one side before realizing his new friend was right behind him. With no time to spare, Connor shoved him out of the kick's path.

Nike's foot struck the wall instead. Incensed, he turned on Connor and launched a furious succession of spinning kicks. Surprised at the boy's skill, Connor was forced to retreat. As he backed away, only instinct—born from hours of sparring—warned him of a simultaneous attack from behind. Glancing over his shoulder, he saw Hoodie step forward and swing the skateboard at his head.

At the last second, Connor ducked. The tail of the deck missed him by a whisker and struck Nike full in the face instead. The boy fell to his knees, semi-concussed.

Hoodie, horrified at his mistake, was now an open target. Connor took advantage and shot out a side kick. But the boy reacted faster than Connor expected and held up his deck as a shield. Having broken wooden blocks to pass his black-belt grading, Connor knew the right technique. Gritting his teeth, he drove on through—the board shattering rather than his foot. From there, it took Connor a simple palm strike to floor Hoodie.

With all three boys out of action, the girl now advanced on him.

Connor held up his hands in peace. "Listen, I don't fight girls. Just walk away and we can forget all about this."

The girl stopped, tilted her head and smiled sweetly at him. "How nice of you."

Then she punched Connor straight in the mouth, splitting his lip. With barely a pause, the girl followed through with a kick to the thigh, her heavy Dr. Martens giving him a dead leg exactly where Jet had struck him earlier in the bout. He crumpled against the wall.

"I fight boys, though!" she said as Connor, stunned and hurting, tried to recover his balance.

The girl went to kick him again, but rather than retreat, Connor moved in and caught her leg in midswing. Struggling to free herself, she sliced the edge of her hand at his neck. But Connor grabbed hold of her wrist and twisted her arm into a lock, forcing her to submit. The girl squealed in pain.

"LET THAT GIRL GO!"

Connor glanced back down the alley. Two police officers— a tall black man and a slender white woman—were hurrying toward them. Connor reluctantly released the girl, who promptly kicked him in the shin before running off in the opposite direction. The rest of the gang followed close on her heels.

Connor went to go after them, but the policeman seized him by the scruff of the neck. "Not so fast, sonny. You're coming with us."

"But I was trying to save this boy," Connor protested.

"What boy?" questioned the policewoman.

Connor looked up and down the alley . . . but it was deserted. The boy had gone.

The officers escorted Connor across Freemasons Road and down a side street to an imposing redbrick building. As they neared the entrance, the traditional blue lamp of the Metropolitan Police came into view. Below this was a sign in bold white lettering declaring Canning Town Police Station. They climbed the steps, passing a poster warning Terrorism— If You Suspect It, Report It, and entered through a set of heavy wooden doors, the blue paint chipped and worn.

The station's foyer was poorly lit and depressingly drab, the walls bare, apart from a bulletin board promoting a local Neighborhood Watch meeting. The sole pieces of furniture were a bench and a glass reception booth, manned by a single bored custody officer. As the three of them approached, he looked up and tutted upon seeing Connor's split lip and the splashes of blood dotted across his sweatshirt.

"Name?" the custody officer asked him.

"Connor Reeves."

He noted this in a ledger. "Address and contact number?"

Connor gave his home in Leytonstone.

"Family?"

"Just my mum and gran," he replied.

As this was added to the ledger, the policewoman explained the reason for detaining Connor, and the custody officer nodded, seemingly satisfied.

"In there," he said, pointing with his pen to a door labeled Interview Room.

Connor was marched across the foyer. The policeman stayed behind to log the contents of his duffel bag with the custody officer.

"After you," said the policewoman, ushering him through.

Connor stepped inside. In the center of the room was a large desk with a single lamp and a couple of hard wooden chairs. A single fluorescent strip buzzed like a mosquito, casting a bleached light over the depressing scene. There was a musty smell in the air, and the blinds were drawn across the window, giving an unsettling sense of isolation from the rest of the world.

In spite of his innocence, Connor's throat went dry with apprehension, and his heart began to beat faster.

This just isn't right! he thought. He'd tried to stop a

mugging and *he* was the one being arrested. And what thanks had he gotten for stepping in? None. The boy had disappeared without a trace.

"Sit down," ordered the policewoman, pointing to the chair in front of the desk.

Connor reluctantly did as he was told.

The policeman rejoined them, closing the door behind him. He handed his colleague a thick folder. The female officer stepped behind the desk, flicked on the lamp and sat opposite Connor. In its glare, Connor watched the policewoman lay the folder on the table and, next to this, place a notepad and pen. To Connor's growing unease, the folder was stamped Strictly Confidential.

He started to sweat. He'd never been in trouble with the police before. *What could they possibly have on me?*

The officer carefully undid the folder's string fastening and began to inspect the file. The towering policeman took up position next to his colleague and stared unflinchingly at Connor. The tension became almost unbearable.

After what seemed an age, the policewoman declared, "If that girl files a charge against you—for assault—it would be a matter for the courts."

Connor felt the ground beneath him give way. This was turning out to be far more serious than he could have ever imagined.

"So we need to take a full statement from you," she explained.

"Shouldn't I call a lawyer or something?" Connor asked, knowing that's what was always said in the movies.

"No, that won't be necessary," replied the officer. "Just tell us why you did it."

Connor shifted uneasily in his seat. "Because . . . there was a boy being mugged."

The police officer made a note. "Did you know this boy?"

"No," replied Connor. "And I never will. The ungrateful kid ran away."

"So why decide to get involved in the first place?"

"They were calling him names and about to beat him up!"

"But other people walked on by. Why didn't you?"

Connor shrugged. "It was the right thing to do. He couldn't stand up for himself. It was four against one."

"Four?" repeated the police officer, jotting down more notes. "Yet you took them on alone."

Connor nodded, conceding, "I know a bit of martial arts."

The officer flicked through the files. "It says here you're a black belt in kickboxing and jujitsu. I don't call that just a bit."

Connor's breath caught in his throat. *How come the officer has this information to hand? What else do they know?*

"That's . . . right," he admitted, wondering if this would count against him. His instructors had always warned him to be careful about using his skills outside the dojo.

"So let's get the story straight," said the policewoman, putting down her pen and looking Connor squarely in the eye. "You're saying you put your life at risk for a complete stranger."

Connor hesitated. *Am I about to plead guilty to an offense?*

"Well . . . yes," he confessed.

A hint of a smile passed across the policewoman's lips. "That takes guts," she said approvingly.

Connor stared in astonishment at the policewoman's unexpected praise. The officer closed her file, then looked up at the policeman and nodded.

He turned to Connor. "Well done—you've passed."

Connor's brow furrowed in bewilderment. "Passed *what*?"

"The Test."

"You mean . . . like a school exam or something?"

"No," he replied. "Real-life combat."

Connor was now even more confused. "Are you saying that gang was a *test* for me?"

The policeman nodded. "You displayed instinctive protection skills."

"Of course I did!" he exclaimed, feeling his frustration rise. "The gang attacked me—"

"That's not what we mean," interrupted the police-woman. "You showed a natural willingness to defend *another* person."

Connor got up from his seat. "What's going on here? I want to call home."

"There's no need," she said, offering a friendly smile. "We've already informed your mother that you may be running a little late."

Connor's mouth fell open in disbelief. *What on earth are the police up to?*

"We've had our eye on you for some time," revealed the policewoman, rising from her chair and perching on the side of the desk, her manner becoming more relaxed and informal. "The attack was set up to test your moral code and combat skills. It had to be authentic, which meant we couldn't warn you. That's why we used trained operatives for the assignment."

Trained operatives? thought Connor, putting a hand to his split lip. *No wonder they were so skilled at fighting.*

"But why?" he demanded.

"We needed to assess your potential to be a CPO in the real world."

Connor blinked in surprise, wondering if he'd heard right. "A what?"

"A close-protection officer," explained the policeman. "By

placing yourself in harm's way to protect another, you proved you have the natural instinct of a bodyguard. You can't teach that. It has to be part of who you are."

Connor laughed at the idea. "You can't be serious! I'm too young to be a bodyguard."

"That's *exactly* the point," replied a voice from behind him in a clipped military tone.

Connor spun around and was shocked to find the silver-haired man from the tournament standing right behind him.

"With training, you'll make the *perfect* bodyguard."

4

"My name is Colonel Black," the man said, introducing himself with a curt nod. Dressed in pristine chinos, polished black boots and a khaki shirt, the sleeves rolled up to the elbows, his appearance conveyed a life spent in the military. Up close, Connor could see the man had craggy features and a strong, chiseled jaw. His demeanor was at once disciplined and authoritative, his flint-gray eyes never wavering from Connor's face. And although he looked to be in his late forties, he possessed the physique of a man ten years younger—broad-chested with tanned, muscular forearms. Only a ragged white scar cutting a line across his throat detracted from this flawless image, no doubt the result of active service.

"I was most impressed with your performance today, both in and out of the ring," he said. "You displayed true grit. Even when the odds were stacked against you, you didn't give up. I like that in a recruit."

"Thank you," replied Connor, too bewildered to say anything else. Then the colonel's words hit home. "What do you mean, *recruit*?"

"Take a seat and I'll explain."

His invitation wasn't quite an order, but Connor felt compelled to sit down anyway. The colonel walked around to the other side of the desk and took over the proceedings from the two police officers.

"I head up a close-protection organization known as Guardian."

"*Guardian*?" Connor shrugged. "Never heard of it."

"Few people have. It's a highly secretive operation," the colonel explained. "So, before I continue, I must stress that this information is classified in the interests of national security and not to be repeated—to *anyone*."

The stern expression on the colonel's face left Connor no room for doubt that there'd be grave repercussions if he ever did. "I understand," he replied.

The colonel took him at his word and continued. "In today's world, there's a demand for a new breed of bodyguard. The constant threat of terrorism, the growth of criminal gangs and the surge in pirate attacks all mean an increased risk of hostage-taking, blackmail and assassination. And, with the overt media coverage of politicians' families, the rise of teen pop stars and the new wave of billionaires, adults are not the only target—children are too."

"You mean like that French movie star's son?" interrupted Connor. The story of the boy's kidnapping while on a sailing vacation had been splashed all over the news.

"Yes, they ended up paying a million dollars for his safe return. But it needn't have happened in the first place—and wouldn't have if the family had employed a close-protection team. And my organization provides just such a service. Yet it differs from all other security outfits by training and supplying only *young* bodyguards." Colonel Black looked directly at Connor as he said this. "These highly skilled individuals are often more effective than typical adult bodyguards, who can easily draw unwanted attention. Operating invisibly as the child's constant companion, a guardian provides the greatest possible protection for any vulnerable or high-profile target."

The colonel paused to allow everything he'd said to sink in.

"And you want *me* to become a guardian?" said Connor dubiously.

"You've got it in one."

Connor laughed uneasily and held up his hands in objection. "You've made a mistake. You must have the wrong person."

The colonel shook his head. "I don't think so."

"But I'm still in school. I can't be a bodyguard!"

"Why not? It's in your blood."

Connor gave Colonel Black a baffled look. Then the colonel said something that completely threw him.

"You'll be following in your father's footsteps."

"What are you talking about?" shot back Connor, suddenly going on the defensive. "My dad's dead."

The colonel nodded solemnly. "I'm aware of that. And I was very much grieved when I heard the news. Your father and I were close friends. We fought together."

Connor studied the man before him, wondering if he was telling the truth. "But my dad never mentioned you."

"That's understandable. In the SAS, we try to keep our personal and professional lives separate."

"Special Air Service? My dad was in the army, Royal Signals," Connor corrected him.

"That was his cover job. Your father was actually in the SAS Special Projects Team, responsible for counterterrorism and VIP close protection," the colonel revealed. "One of the best."

This new knowledge unsettled Connor, who thought he'd known his father pretty well. "Then why did he never tell me that?"

"As a member of Special Projects, your father had to keep his identity secret. To protect himself, you and the rest of your family."

"I don't believe you," said Connor, gripping the arm of his chair for support. His whole world seemed to be shifting sideways as the long-held memory of his father was brought into question.

The colonel removed a photo from his breast pocket and handed it to Connor.

"Iraq, 2004."

Five soldiers in combat fatigues and carrying submachine guns stood before a barren patch of desert scrub. In the middle was a younger Colonel Black, his distinctive scar visible just above the neckline of his body armor. Next to him was a tall, tanned man with dark brown hair and familiar green-blue eyes—Justin Reeves.

Connor was speechless. Gripping the photograph with a trembling hand, he fought back the tears at seeing his father's face so unexpectedly.

"You can keep that if you want," said the colonel. "Now, on to your recruitment into Guardian."

"What?" Connor exclaimed, events moving too fast for him. "But I haven't agreed to anything."

"True. But hear me out and you will."

Connor tentatively put his father's photo down on the desk, reluctant to let it out of his sight.

"First, your school will be informed of your transfer to a private school."

"*Private* school?" Connor asked. "My family doesn't have that sort of money."

"You'll be funded by a special scholarship scheme. Besides,

we need an official cover for your relocation to the Guardian training camp. We must maintain the secrecy of our operation. No one can *ever* know."

"Relocation?" challenged Connor. "I'm sorry, but I can't leave my mum. You'll have to find someone else."

"We're aware of your situation," said the policewoman with a reassuring smile as she placed an envelope on the table for him. "We've made all the necessary arrangements to ensure she's well looked after. And all the costs are covered."

Connor stared at the mysterious envelope, then at Colonel Black. "What if I don't want to become a bodyguard?"

"It's entirely your decision. You're free to go home, but I think you'll regret it."

A truth suddenly dawned on Connor. "So I'm not under arrest?"

"Whoever said you were?" replied the colonel, arching an eyebrow.

Connor turned to the two police officers, then realized that neither of them had read him his rights or *officially* arrested him. They'd only asked him to accompany them to the station.

"I'll leave you to think about my offer," said Colonel Black, laying a business card on top of the envelope. The card was black as night with an embossed silver logo of a shield sprouting wings. Below it was a single telephone number— and nothing else.

The colonel nodded good-bye, then disappeared out through the door, the two police officers in tow.

Connor was left alone in the room. He stared at the card, his mind whirling with the events of the past hour. His life had been spun on its axis—one moment he was being crowned UK Kickboxing Champion, the next he was being recruited as a bodyguard. He stared at the envelope, both intrigued and a bit afraid of what it might contain. He decided to leave it for later. He had other matters to think about first.

Picking up the card, the envelope and the photo of his father, Connor stood and headed for the door. When he opened it, he thought he'd made a mistake and gone the wrong way. The lights in the foyer were all off, and the reception booth was deserted, the building silent as a grave.

"Hello? Anyone there?" he called. But no one answered.

He spotted his duffel bag on the counter. Stowing the envelope and photo next to his trophy and pocketing the colonel's business card, he made his way to the main entrance. His footsteps echoed through the empty foyer. As he passed the bulletin board, he saw that the Neighborhood Watch meeting had been two years ago and briefly wondered why the announcement was still up. Pushing open the heavy double doors, he stepped outside into the gray evening light. Relieved to escape the tomb-like atmosphere of the station, he looked down the street for Colonel Black. But neither the colonel nor the police officers were in sight.

Then, as the double doors slammed shut behind him, he noticed the terrorism poster had been taken down. An official blue-and-white sign was now visible:

NOTICE

THIS IS
NO LONGER
A POLICE STATION

THE NEAREST
STATION IS
444 BARKING
ROAD, PLAISTOW

Connor stared at the sign, stunned. The whole operation had been a setup!

He felt in his pocket and pulled out the one thing proving the encounter had even occurred—the black business card with the silver winged shield . . . and a solitary telephone number.

5

"You're late, Hazim," the brooding man growled in Arabic through a mouthful of green khat leaves. The man, who boasted a thick, bushy beard, a hooked nose and sun-blasted skin the color of the deep desert, bared a row of brownish-yellow teeth in displeasure.

"I'm sorry, Malik, but the plane was delayed getting in," replied Hazim, bowing his head in deference to the man who sat like a king at the far end of the rectangular white-washed *mafraj* room.

Malik tutted in irritation, yet nonetheless waved him over to sit by his side. Hazim, a young man of Yemeni origin with dominant eyebrows and an angular face, almost handsome if not for his downturned mouth, nervously took his place among the other members of the Brotherhood.

The room was full of men dressed in ankle-length *thawb*, their white cotton robes providing relief from the heat of the day. Some were bareheaded, others wore red-and-white-checkered headscarves. They reclined on large cushions, left leg tucked underneath, right arm upon the right knee, and the left arm supported by a padded armrest. Before each was a pile of green stems from which they picked leaves to chew as they engaged in animated conversation.

As was tradition in a *mafraj* room, there were two rows of windows, the upper set decorated in stained glass through which the late-afternoon sun scattered shards of rainbow colors across the thickly carpeted floor. The lower clear windows were pushed wide open to allow a cool breeze to waft in. Not accustomed to the country's intense heat, Hazim turned toward one of the openings in relief. From the topmost floor of the house, he was able to admire the magnificent vista of Sana'a, the capital city of Yemen. The flat sun-dried rooftops of the myriad white and sand-colored houses stretched into the distance, where they met the awe-inspiring Sarawat mountain range.

"Where's your khat?" demanded Malik.

Hazim held up his hands in apology. "Sorry. I was more worried about the CIA trailing me than shopping in the souk."

"Tsk!" Malik spat, batting away his excuse. "I won't tolerate lateness or lack of respect for our traditions. Understand?"

Hazim nodded, shifting uncomfortably under the man's

fierce gaze. Then, like quicksilver, Malik's harsh expression switched to a genial smile, and he clapped Hazim on the back.

"No matter this time, Hazim. You were right to be cautious. Kedar, give him some of yours," he ordered a man to Hazim's left. "A true Yemeni should never be without."

Kedar, a man of Herculean build with a wiry beard, offered Hazim a handful of green stems. Chewing khat was the social norm in Yemen. All men gathered together at the end of the day to sit down, chew khat and put the world to rights, just as Americans met in Starbucks for coffee and the English enjoyed a pot of tea—except the effect of chewing khat was the equivalent of several strong espressos in a row.

Nodding gratefully to Kedar, Hazim pulled a few leaves from a stem and popped them into his mouth. As he bit down, the bitterness of the khat's juices hit his taste buds.

"Do you have a Coke?" he asked, trying not to grimace.

Malik threw up his arms in exaggerated outrage and turned to a man with thinning hair and rounded scholarly glasses. "This is what I mean, Bahir! The poison of America seeps into his bones. There's fine Yemeni water over there," he muttered, indicating a large ceramic jug on a round wooden table. "The only and *proper* way to enjoy khat."

Selecting the choicest leaves from his bundle, Malik

stuffed several into his left cheek at once. He chewed slowly, carefully studying Hazim as the young man poured a glass for himself. "He doesn't even have a beard!" he snorted.

Sipping on his water, Hazim self-consciously put a hand to his shaven face and glanced around at his bearded brethren. The other men all eyed him guardedly.

"He looks like a newborn," commented Bahir. "Hey, everyone, it's Baby Hazim!"

The group burst into raucous laughter. Hazim flushed in humiliation and cast his eyes to the floor. But the jesting was ultimately good-natured, for all in the room knew the truth. Hazim had been invited into the inner circle of the Brotherhood precisely because he'd shown he *was* able to integrate effortlessly into American life.

Malik patted Hazim reassuringly on the shoulder. "Enough! Now we're all here, we can begin," he announced.

The laughter of the other men died quickly, all conversation coming to a halt.

"My brothers," he began, opening his arms wide. "Our organization has hidden in the shadows long enough. The time is ripe for a nightmare attack against our enemy. The toppling of the Twin Towers struck at the heart of America. Now I intend for us to destroy its soul!"

Malik fingered his prize *jambiya* as he spoke. The curved dagger was thrust into his leather belt, positioned in full view of everyone. The semiprecious stones adorning the wooden sheath glistened in the evening's fading light, and with its handle of rare rhinoceros horn, no man would question his status as leader. Whereas for most Yemeni men the *jambiya* was purely a symbol of masculinity and usually blunt, Malik kept his blade sharpened, having used it to slit many an enemy's throat.

"We must hit America where it hurts the most," he continued, his fervor building. "A wise man once said, 'Kill a few, hurt many, scare thousands.' But in this attack, we need only kidnap *one* infidel."

He paused, relishing the moment of power as his men leaned in, mesmerized by his words.

"Who's the target?" breathed Bahir.

"The president's daughter."

A round of gasps met this revelation. Not from disgust, but from admiration at the audacity of the plan.

But Hazim couldn't hide his skepticism. "You seriously intend for us to *kidnap* the president's daughter? One of the most protected families in the world."

"Yes," said Malik smugly. "The plan may be bold, but it'll be as devastating and effective as a thousand bombs. Once we have her, we'll demand the release of our brothers and force all infidels to leave our lands."

The men cheered at this news, pumping their fists in the air. Hazim tried to get himself heard over the hubbub. "The United States doesn't negotiate with those they label terrorists. What makes you think the president will bow to our demands?"

Malik removed his *jambiya* and inspected the gleaming blade. "What father wouldn't if you held his own flesh and blood hostage?"

6

Connor's thumb hovered over the Call button of his phone. The telephone number glowed steadily in the display, but he couldn't quite bring himself to dial it.

Am I doing the right thing?

He could hear his mum shuffling around downstairs, making them breakfast. Connor wondered if she'd manage on her own. The TV was on in the sitting room, the volume a notch too high for Connor's comfort, to compensate for his gran's failing hearing. But no one complained; their neighbors were just as old, and only the three of them lived in the house.

Spread out on his bed were the contents of the envelope: a company brochure promoting high-quality live-in caregivers for the elderly and chronically ill, plus a letter detailing Colonel Black's offer. Connor knew exactly what it said. And each time he read the letter, it made more sense.

His mum suffered from multiple sclerosis. On a day-to-day basis, he looked after her, helped by his gran. But when he was at school or martial arts training, he couldn't be around. And recently there'd been a couple of incidents that had worried him—the dropping of a pan of boiling water, then a painful fall down the stairs that had resulted in a broken wrist. As his mum's condition worsened, she'd need full-time care.

On top of that, he'd noticed his gran was finding it harder to cope. Although her mind was still sharp as a tack, she was getting old and less mobile. As a family, they'd once discussed the idea of nursing homes. But his gran had been adamant it would be the death of her. The little terraced house was full of happy memories of her life with his grandad and father, and she was determined to stay. For his mum's part, she was more worried about what would happen to her son if she was forced to go into a nursing home. Being a minor, Connor couldn't remain in the house alone. And without any close relatives his choices seemed limited to foster care or entering a children's home himself—prospects that appealed to neither him nor his mother.

Their ideal solution was a live-in caregiver. But there was no way they could afford one.

Until now.

Connor had spent the past week deliberating over the

decision. He dearly loved his mum and gran and didn't want to leave them. Yet by joining Guardian he would guarantee their well-being. And he considered it his duty to look after them, just as they'd looked after *him* when his father had died.

He glanced over at the photo on the bedside table of his father in Iraq. Six years had gone by, but there wasn't a day when Connor didn't think of him. His memories were now like snapshots in a dusty family album—playing soccer in the park, games of hide-and-seek in Epping Forest, sparring in their backyard. And with each passing year these snapshots faded a little more. Connor was worried that one day he wouldn't be able to recall his father at all.

But Colonel Black and his father had been friends. He could fill in the missing pieces. And Connor desperately wanted to know more about his father's secret life—what it was like being in the SAS and working as a bodyguard in hostile environments. He also needed to understand why his father had devoted himself to such a job, one that took him away from his family for such long periods. Connor realized he could never get his father back, but by following in his footsteps he *might* come to know him better.

Connor pressed the Call button.

It rang once before being answered in that familiar clipped tone.

"Glad you've decided to join us," said the colonel. "One

of the team will collect you Monday at 0900 hours sharp. Be ready."

"But . . . I-I still haven't agreed to anything yet," Connor stuttered.

He sensed a smile at the other end of the line.

"Connor, you wouldn't be calling *unless* it was to say yes."

7

The following Monday a blacked-out Range Rover pulled up outside the house: 0900 hours sharp.

Bags packed, Connor hugged his mum good-bye. "I'll be back during the holidays," he promised.

"Now, don't you worry about me," she said, kissing him tenderly on the cheek. "You go have a good time. I'm so proud of you."

She squeezed his hand. To Connor, his mother always seemed at her most energized and pain-free when she was concentrating on him.

"And I'll be here 24/7," reassured Sally, a jolly, middle-aged woman who was to be his mum's live-in caregiver.

The morning after the phone call, Sally had dropped by their house. Over a pot of tea, she'd explained the in-home care arrangement and said the costs were being covered by Connor's "scholarship program." His mum had immediately warmed to the idea, proud that her son's talents were being recognized. By the second cup of tea, the three women were swapping stories and laughing like old friends. Reassured, Connor knew his mother was in good hands and that he'd made the right decision for her.

And it had the double benefit that his gran would also be cared for in her own home. This news had initially pleased his gran. But, not one to miss a trick, she had questioned him in private about the "scholarship program." Despite Colonel Black's warning, Connor had told her the truth—as he always did with his gran. She'd immediately tried to dissuade him. But, seeing the determination in his eyes, she'd resignedly shaken her head and said, "You're your father's son. Always putting others before yourself."

So it was agreed that Guardian was to be their secret, and Connor had no doubt that she'd keep it. As he went to say good-bye, his gran gripped him with surprising strength.

"Stay safe," she whispered, and for a moment he didn't think she'd let him go.

With a final hug for his mum, Connor picked up his bags and strode over to the Range Rover. The driver got out, a slender woman with dark brown shoulder-length hair and olive eyes that were good-natured yet watchful.

Connor smiled in wry recognition. "You're not going to arrest me again, are you?"

The former policewoman laughed. "Only if you don't pay attention in class!" She offered her hand. "I'm Jody, one of your instructors. Now get in. We've got a long drive ahead."

Connor tossed his bags into the trunk and clambered into the passenger seat. With a last wave to his mum and gran, he heaved the door shut and the Range Rover pulled away. As they drove out of London, they passed the Tiger Martial Arts Dojo. Connor felt a twinge of regret, and a nagging doubt returned. The club was almost a second home to him. He'd just made his mark as a national kickboxing champion. *Am I throwing it all away?* His instructor hadn't thought so. Although dismayed to lose his most promising student, Dan had only wanted the best for him.

"The time to strike is when the opportunity presents itself," Dan had said, giving him a friendly tap on the chin with his fist. "So good luck—and remember: if you get into trouble, *hit first, hit hard, then hit the ground running.*"

The Range Rover turned a corner and the club disappeared from view. Burying his doubts, Connor now felt an undeniable thrill at what lay in store for him as a bodyguard. "So where are we going?" he asked eagerly.

"Wales," replied Jody.

"Oh." Connor tried to hide his disappointment. He'd been expecting somewhere a little more glamorous. "Why there?"

"You'll find out soon enough," she replied. "Until then, I'd advise getting some rest while you can. The weeks ahead will be demanding."

Leaving London, they headed west on the M4 motorway.

While Jody drove, Connor asked her about the Guardian organization—a search on the Internet had drawn a blank, apart from a news clipping mentioning Colonel Black as the team leader of a high-profile hostage rescue in Afghanistan several years before. But Jody politely evaded this line of questioning. "All will be answered in good time," she replied. After his fifth attempt to extract information, she flashed him a steely look and he backed off. However, Jody did reveal that she was an ex–police officer of some fifteen years' service. Rapidly promoted up the ranks, she'd moved to CO19, the police's specialist armed unit, before being transferred to SO14, Royalty Close Protection.

"So did you ever protect Prince William and Kate Middleton?" Connor asked.

Jody's manner became guarded again. "That would break client confidentiality, I'm afraid."

Finding it was like getting blood from a stone, Connor decided to take her earlier advice and tried to sleep.

Three hours later, they crossed the Severn Bridge into Wales. When they eventually came off the highway, Jody took so many minor roads that Connor lost his bearings completely. But judging by the craggy mountains and endless fields, they were in the middle of nowhere.

It was late afternoon by the time a pair of iron gates came into view. Atop the black wrought-iron design was a subtle but distinctive winged shield. Leveling with an entry port concealed in the bushes, Jody pressed an infrared sensor on the dashboard and the gates parted. As they drove through, Connor spotted a discreet security camera following their progress. The Range Rover crunched up a long gravel driveway with open fields on either side. As they crested a rise, an old granite building appeared, not visible from the road. The size of a country mansion, it was tucked into its own valley with a small lake and dense patch of woodland. Squared battlements and narrow windows gave the impression of a fortified castle.

"This was a private school in the 1800s," explained Jody. "But the facilities have been updated for our purposes."

To Connor, the school still looked as if it belonged in the nineteenth century, and he struggled to see much improvement beyond a large satellite dish on the roof.

The Range Rover drew up outside the main entrance. Connor jumped out and retrieved his bags from the trunk. When he turned around, he almost dropped them. Standing in the arched doorway was the *last* person he had expected to see.

8

"Welcome to Camp Guardian!" said the boy he'd tried to rescue in the alley. Helping Connor with his bags, he introduced himself. "My name's Amir."

"So this is where you ran off to," remarked Connor.

Amir offered a ready smile. "Yeah, sorry I didn't get a chance to thank you, but I thought Jody was about to arrest me for late coursework." He shot the instructor a mischievous wink.

"Show our new recruit to his room," Jody ordered, apparently immune to his charm.

Amir performed an overzealous salute. "Yes, ma'am."

Shorter than Connor and with a lean frame, Amir bounded up the steps into the school's entrance hall. His exuberant manner reminded Connor of a meerkat's—playful yet always on the alert. He was a totally different person from the cowering victim Connor had come across in the Docklands.

"And, Amir," Jody called after them, her tone stern, "I want that threat report on my desk by 0800 hours."

Groaning at the deadline, Amir turned to Connor. "Let's go before she makes it any earlier."

He led Connor through a grand entrance hall and up a wide, sweeping staircase. Old paintings in antique frames hung from the walls, and the last of the sun's rays filtered through a bay window onto the polished parquet flooring.

"So you're a guardian?" said Connor as they climbed the stairs to the third floor.

Amir nodded. "Trainee. I've not been on any assignments yet, so I haven't earned my wings." He pointed to a silver lapel badge on his sweater, the familiar shield and silhouette absent of its Guardian wings. "But hopefully it won't be long. Just depends on who the next Principal is."

"*Principal*?" asked Connor.

"The person you're assigned to protect," explained Amir, turning right along a corridor. "It could be a politician's son, a member of a royal family, the daughter of an oil baron, anyone who is likely to be a target of an attack." He nudged Connor with a conspiratorial elbow. "To be honest, I'm hoping for a film star. Now, that would be cool. All those red carpet events!"

He pointed to an open door on their left. "That's my room, by the way."

Connor glimpsed an unmade bed with clothes strewn

everywhere and a small desk upon which sat a gutted laptop. "What happened to your computer?" he asked.

"Nothing. Just updating the hard drive and installing a new multicore processor," Amir replied, as if such a task was as easy as replacing a lightbulb.

He stopped by a door marked with a number seven.

"This is your room," he announced, inviting Connor to go in first.

The bedroom was small and basic, comprising a desk, chair, lamp, single bed, sink and old wooden wardrobe. Connor dumped his bags on the bed. "I thought Jody said the school had been modernized."

Amir laughed. "It's what you *don't* see that's impressive." He flicked open a panel on the desk to reveal an Internet port. "The whole place is wired with fiber-optic broadband. It's a closed system so no one can access it externally." He pointed to the window. "The glass has shock detectors in case someone tries to break in. Outside, there are covert security cameras, thermal-imaging cameras and pressure pads at every entry and exit. And beyond that there are perimeter alarms surrounding the school grounds."

Connor looked out across the open fields, deserted apart from a flock of windswept sheep. "Why the high-tech security? This isn't exactly a thriving metropolis."

"There's no point in protecting others if we can't protect ourselves," replied Amir. "That's one of the basic rules of bodyguarding. Also, only a handful of people know about Guardian's existence—that's one reason why we're so effective—and Colonel Black wants to keep it that way."

Stuck in the middle of Wales, Connor wondered if the colonel wasn't being a little paranoid. "Then we should watch out for those terrorist sheep!"

Amir responded with a dry chuckle. "Just wait till you start training. You'll be stunned at what lengths the enemy will go to." He glanced at Connor's backpack. "Have you brought a laptop?"

Connor shook his head. He only had an old, battered PC at home.

"Don't worry, I'll figure out how to get you one tomorrow." A phone pinged in Amir's back pocket. "That means dinner's served. You must be starving after the journey."

Making their way downstairs, they headed through to the dining hall. Fifteen or so boys and girls were gathered at one end, sitting at circular tables, chatting and eating. To their left was an open serving area, steaming with freshly cooked food. Passing Connor a tray, Amir grabbed a large plate and helped himself. Connor's mouth watered at the impressive spread of pasta, chicken, curry, rice and even steak.

"This is *nothing* like the school meals I've had before," he remarked, shoveling a mound of fries to go with his rib-eye and mushrooms.

"The colonel believes an army marches on its stomach,"

Amir replied, taking a pineapple juice from the cooler. "And trust me, you'll need the energy!"

With plates piled high, Amir led Connor over to a table nearest the window, where four other recruits sat.

"You remember Jason?" said Amir, arching an eyebrow at Connor.

A broad-chested boy turned around. With dark tousled hair and an anvil jaw, Connor couldn't forget his face . . . or his fists.

"G'day!" said Jason, an Aussie twang now noticeable in his speech. He offered one of his hammer-like fists in greeting. Connor took it and was subjected to a bone-crushing handshake.

I'm off to a great start here! thought Connor, trying not to wince. "You're Australian, then?"

"He sure is! But don't hold that against him," teased the girl perched next to Jason and half his size. She'd lost her emo makeup and was now dressed in jeans, sneakers and a red sleeveless T-shirt, but there was no mistaking that she was the one who'd busted his lip in the alley. "I'm Ling. How's the leg?" she asked with an impish twinkle in her eyes.

"Fine," said Connor, releasing himself from Jason's iron grip. "How's the arm?"

Ling smirked. "Not as bad as you'd have ended up, if Jody hadn't saved you."

"Saved *me*?" Connor responded, remembering the situation differently, but Amir cut in.

"I wouldn't argue with Ling. She *always* wins her fights." He sat down beside the boy with bleached-blond hair. "This is Marc; he's from France."

Marc had replaced the gang fashion with a more stylish Ralph Lauren shirt and white jeans. Dark shadows circled his eyes, the aftereffect of his bruising encounter with the skateboard.

"*Bonsoir,*" he greeted, then with only the trace of a French accent asked, "How was the journey?"

"Long!" remarked Connor. As he took his place next to Amir, his eyes were drawn to the girl sitting opposite him. Perhaps a year older than the others, with tanned skin, sun-kissed blond hair and a radiant smile, she looked like she'd just stepped off a Caribbean beach. She wore a black halter-neck top with a winged-shield badge in *gold*.

"I hear you beat Jason," she said in a soft American accent like honey. "That's a first."

"I held back," Jason growled in protest. "Didn't want to hurt the newbie."

The girl gave a noncommittal nod. "Of course you did!" she said, smirking.

In an effort to smooth over his rocky start with Jason, Connor interjected, "Well, to be fair . . . he did telegraph that first punch."

"Exactly," agreed Jason, a little too quickly.

The girl glanced at Connor, her sky-blue eyes appraising him. Seeing straight through his white lie, the corner of her mouth curled up into a knowing smile. "I'm Charlotte. But everyone calls me Charley."

Connor smiled back, hoping the flush in his cheeks wasn't noticeable. He was usually fine around girls. But for some reason, this one made him feel a touch self-conscious. Opting for a safe opening question, he asked, "Where in the States are you from?"

"California," she replied. "The Guardian gathers recruits from around the world." She pointed to the other tables. "For example, José is from Mexico, Elsa from Germany, David from Uganda, Luciana from Brazil."

Connor glanced around the hall, the tables only half full. "Are these *all* the guardians?"

Charley shook her head. "Most are on assignment. But no more than twenty of us are usually here at any one time."

"So where's the skater boy who attacked me?"

"Richie's in Ireland," Amir replied, through a mouthful of rice.

"*Bonne chose aussi*," mumbled Marc, massaging the bridge of his nose.

"Sorry, what was that?" said Connor, wishing he'd paid more attention in his French class.

"Good thing too," Marc repeated. "I might have forgiven him by the time he gets back."

"So that means, Connor, you'll be joining us in Alpha team," Charley announced. "By the way, the colonel wants us all in the briefing room at 0800 hours. After fitness training."

Marc let out a heavy sigh. "I hate six a.m. cross-country runs."

Connor raised his eyebrows at this remark. He didn't mind running, but he agreed with Marc—not *before* breakfast.

"And I still have a threat report to complete!" Amir complained, stabbing his chicken with a fork.

"Best get on with it, then," suggested Charley, offering little sympathy.

"I warn you, Connor," said Marc, picking up his tray to go, "Guardian is *no* holiday camp."

The others stood to leave too. Apart from Charley. She rolled back her wheelchair before heading for the door.

Taken by surprise, Connor couldn't help but stare.

Amir noticed his eyes following Charley's exit and whispered, "She was injured on an assignment."

"How?"

"I don't know the details. And Charley prefers not to talk about it."

That evening Connor didn't feel like unpacking. He lay

on his bed, listening to the wind whistling outside. His thoughts turned to Charley and the shock of seeing her using a wheelchair. The reality of what he'd agreed to hit home. Being a bodyguard was no game. The risks were real. *Dangerously real.*

9

"Do you understand what I've tasked you with?" questioned Malik, sitting cross-legged beneath the shade of an olive tree in his courtyard garden on the outskirts of Sana'a. Laid out on a cloth before the leader was a large bowl of *saltah* stew, a plate of *aseed* dried fish with cheese, boiled rice, *malooga* flatbread and a pot of black tea.

Hazim nodded. "I'm honored to be entrusted so."

Malik smiled the thin grin of a snake. "You've been chosen, Hazim, because of your rather unique position. No one among the Brotherhood can get as close to the president's daughter as you. But nothing can be left to chance. Our planning must be meticulous and our methods discreet."

"I understand."

"You must tell no one of your true purpose. Especially your family."

"I won't," assured Hazim, "although *you're* family, Uncle."

Malik barked a desert-dry laugh. "And that's why I trust you, Hazim. You're like a son to me."

Hazim beamed with pride. "You've always shown me favor, Uncle. It was you who encouraged my studies at the mosque in the first place. And that's why I won't let you down."

"I trust not," said Malik, all traces of humor vanishing from his face. "The role you play will be vital. And you'll be provided with all the surveillance resources and backup you need. Bahir is to be responsible for communications and technology, and Kedar for managing our defensive require-ments. Now, do you have any questions?"

Malik paused to take a sip of black tea from a small china cup, giving Hazim the opportunity to speak.

"You say money's no object," began Hazim, "yet how can the Brotherhood fund an operation like this?"

"You need not concern yourself with that," said Malik, his tone hardening. "It doesn't matter what it costs when the prize is so great."

Selecting a piece of flatbread from the plate, Malik scooped up a helping of *saltah* and shoveled the meat stew into his mouth. He chewed slowly as he studied Hazim. "All that's important is that you're willing to do what's necessary for the purpose of achieving our goal."

His coal-black eyes bored into Hazim's as he searched

for the slightest evidence of doubt, any flicker of cowardice.

Hazim held Malik's stare. "I'm well aware of the dangers, Uncle. And I'm resolved to my calling."

Malik grinned in satisfaction, licking the stew from his yellow-stained teeth. "Excellent."

10

"Bodyguards are the modern-day samurai warriors," declared Colonel Black, clicking up an image of a Japanese swordsman on the overhead projector. "Like these ancient warriors, the bodyguard's duty is to protect their Principal above all else."

Connor sat with Alpha team in the briefing room, a windowless chamber at the heart of the school building. Decked out with HD flat-screen projectors, state-of-the-art computers and ergonomic high-backed lecture chairs, it was unlike any classroom Connor had ever been in.

"These warriors followed the code of *bushido*—a set of virtues that shaped the samurai's training and attitude toward life. Today, a professional bodyguard adheres to the same principles of Loyalty, Honor and Courage."

"You're making us sound like heroes!" jested Marc.

"You are," replied the colonel, his gaze briefly falling on Charley sitting in her chair at the front. "But you'll be unsung heroes. Connor, you must forget the Hollywood image of the muscle-bound bouncer in a suit clearing a path for some starlet through a screaming crowd. Or a Secret Service 007-type in dark shades, talking into his sleeve, hand inside his jacket ready to draw a gun at the slightest threat. The best bodyguards are the ones that *nobody* notices."

The next image on the screen showed a restaurant scene. A family of four sat at a table surrounded by other diners.

"Where are the bodyguards in this picture, Connor?"

Connor searched the image for clues. "The obvious one is the big man in the suit standing by the window, but you just said it *can't* be him."

"Correct. He's the restaurant's doorman. The actual protection team is here." The colonel shone a laser pointer at a couple having a seemingly romantic meal. "And also here." The red beam now shone on the young girl at the family table. "She's one of our guardians. And that's why *you've* all been chosen. To blend into the background. To become the unassuming friend. By not drawing attention to your Principal, you reduce the risk of making them a target."

"So why do celebrities always use the Hollywood type?" asked Connor.

"As a deterrent," replied the colonel, picking up a coffee mug and taking a sip. "If the Principal is a film star, for example, high-profile protection will keep any fanatical followers at bay. And, in these cases, generally the bigger and uglier the bodyguard appears, the easier it is for them to do their job."

"Makes Jason perfect for the role!" remarked Ling out of the corner of her mouth.

Jason flicked his pen lid at her. "Careful I don't step on you, Minnie Mouse!"

She caught the lid in midair without looking. "You'll have to be quicker than that to get me."

"Ling!" barked the colonel, bringing a swift end to the frivolity. "I realize Alpha team knows much of this already, but this session is designed to bring Connor up to speed, and the review is beneficial for you too. So tell me, what's the key to effective security as a bodyguard?"

"Constant awareness," Ling replied, her expression turning studious.

The colonel slammed his palm on the lectern. Amir almost leaped from his chair in fright at the sudden noise.

"What did Ling just say, Amir?"

"Um . . . constant . . . awareness," he replied, stifling a yawn. The combination of working late and rising early had clearly taken its toll.

"And you'd do well to remember that," warned the colonel. "If you're aware, you're less likely to be taken by surprise. And that could mean the difference between life and death for both you and your Principal."

"Yes, sir," said Amir, sitting up straight.

"Now explain the relevance of the Cooper Color Code."

Amir swiveled in his chair to face Connor. "According to Marine Lieutenant Colonel Jeff Cooper, the most important means of surviving a lethal confrontation isn't a weapon or martial arts skills but the correct combat mind-set. He identified four levels of awareness—White, Yellow, Orange and Red. Code White means being totally switched off. This is where ninety-five percent of people spend ninety-five percent of their time—living in their own bubble. Like when you're on a smartphone and you cross the road without looking."

Connor nodded, having been guilty of this himself many a time and once almost getting run over.

"Code White is no place for a bodyguard to be," emphasized the colonel. "If you're suddenly attacked, you'll get a massive surge of adrenaline that your body won't be able to cope with. It'll trigger a state of *fight, flight or freeze*. This sensory overload will hinder you from protecting your Principal, who's probably in the same state of shock. You need to be thinking straight, making lightning-fast decisions and taking the appropriate actions to get your Principal out of danger."

The colonel's steely gray eyes fixed on Marc. "So, what state of mind should a bodyguard always be in?"

"Code Yellow—relaxed alertness," replied Marc. "There's no

specific threat, but you're aware that the world's a dangerous place and you're prepared to defend yourself and your Principal, if necessary. You use all your senses to scan the surroundings in a relaxed yet alert manner."

"What's the problem with Code Yellow, Jason?"

Jason looked up from his laptop. Tapping his pen on the lecture chair's writing table, he thought for a moment. "Um . . . Although it's simple enough to 'switch on' and become alert, the difficulty is in maintaining that state. You can easily drift back into Code White without even realizing it."

The colonel raised his eyebrows pointedly at Amir to ensure he got the message. "But with practice you can 'live' in Code Yellow on an indefinite basis. Now, Charley, explain to Connor the last two states of awareness."

"Code Orange is a specific alert. Having noticed a potential threat, you evaluate your choices. Run, fight or wait and see, depending on how the situation develops," she explained fluidly. "Code Red is the trigger. The threat has escalated into a hazardous situation. Having made your decisions in Code Orange, you're now acting on them."

"Exactly," said Colonel Black, pleased with her response. "You haven't jumped from Code White to Code Red in a single leap, resulting in potential 'brain fade.'

"Since your mind-set is already in a heightened state of awareness, your body can handle the rush of adrenaline.

This means you can run faster, hit harder, think quicker and jump higher than you could seconds before."

The colonel directed his gaze toward Connor. "In short, the Color Code helps a bodyguard stay in control and think clearly in a life-threatening situation."

11

Connor was now glad of that early-morning run. His brain was just about "alert" enough to take this information in. As Connor made notes on the laptop Amir had provided, the colonel forwarded the presentation to a silhouette of a young boy surrounded by four concentric circles. Each ring was marked with a different initialism from the outside in: RST, SAP, PES and BG.

"In the majority of assignments, you'll work as part of a larger adult close-protection team," explained Colonel Black. His laser pointer flicked to the outermost circle, RST. "The Residential Security Team, as the name implies, manages the physical security of anywhere your Principal's family might stay—for example, a house, a hotel or a yacht. They'll perform searches, monitor security feeds and check every visitor in and out. In theory, this *should* be the safest place for you and your Principal. On the other hand, being a fixed and known location, a residence is the most obvious target for an attack."

The red beam moved into the SAP circle.

"The Security Advance Party provides the next layer of protection. They travel ahead of the family, checking that routes and venues are safe. This may happen months in advance, say for a vacation—or minutes, in the case of an impromptu visit to a restaurant. Many potential attacks have been foiled by an observant SAP team. Good communication with them is essential—you don't want any surprises when you're out and about."

The PES circle was now highlighted. "The Personal Escort Section provides a crucial layer of defense when the family is on the move. Depending upon the situation, their function may be to provide additional protection or to eliminate a threat and give you time to escape with your Principal."

The colonel's laser pointer spiraled in through the circles once more to reinforce their importance.

"Each of these groups forms a cordon of defense around the Principal and their family." His beam stopped at the smallest innermost circle labeled BG. "But as a guardian you'll be the *final* ring of defense. It's your ultimate responsibility to shield your Principal from danger."

The colonel directed everyone's gaze to the large silver shield and wings hanging over the door of the briefing room. "Hence our logo."

He highlighted three words etched into the burnished metal: *Praedice. Prohibe. Defende.*

"Charley, enlighten Connor with our motto."

"*Predict. Prevent. Protect,*" she recited. "Predict the threat. Prevent the attack. Protect the Principal."

"This isn't a mere saying, Connor," reaffirmed Colonel Black. "This is our method of operation. By identifying a source of danger early, we can minimize the risk of it happening. If we put in place countermeasures, then the Principal will be better protected. Ideally, we'll avoid the threat entirely. For example, if your Principal is a famous young TV star, what threat could she face?"

"A crazed fan?" suggested Connor.

"Very likely. Now, say this crazed fan poses a risk of stabbing to your Principal. How can we prevent this?"

"Body armor," volunteered Amir.

"Effective, but for your Principal to wear body armor all the time is unrealistic and impractical."

"Put a surveillance team on the suspected fan," Ling suggested. "That way you can track their movements and keep the Principal at a safe distance."

"Good. But what if the surveillance team loses the fan?"

"Then the guardian keeps an eye out and provides protection to the Principal," said Jason.

"Exactly. And that's why you need to remain constantly aware—in a Code Yellow mind-set. You have to be continually assessing people who come close enough to harm you or your Principal. Is the person in the crowd reaching for a knife or a gun? Or an innocent smartphone? Have you seen them before? Do they appear unusually nervous? These are the sorts of questions you need to ask yourself."

The colonel paused to take another sip of his coffee.

"Here's a different scenario: your Principal is on a skiing vacation, and there's a demonstration outside her hotel. What action would you take to ensure her safety?"

Connor thought for a moment. "Stay inside until the demonstration moves on."

"That's one option," conceded the colonel, "but your Principal has to meet friends in the next thirty minutes."

Unsure what to suggest, Connor looked to the others for help.

"You could use the PES team to form a protective cordon," said Amir.

"Not ideal," replied the colonel. "Any contact with the demonstration *greatly* increases the risk to your Principal."

Jason put his hand up. "I'd leave by a rear exit."

"Good," Colonel Black agreed. "But your Principal still ends up in the hospital."

"Why?"

"She slips on the icy step of that rarely used exit."

Jason threw up his hands. "How could I predict *that*?"

"You should be on the lookout for *all* dangers," replied the colonel. "This is what I like to call 'salting the step.' When it comes to analyzing the threats against your Principal, leave no stone unturned."

Colonel Black gestured toward Charley.

"As Alpha team's operations leader—and the most experienced guardian among you—Charley will help you predict and prevent any threats against your Principal," he explained. "But it will be up to you *alone* to protect them. And over the coming weeks you'll learn the necessary skills to do just that—unarmed combat, anti-surveillance, body-cover drills and anti-ambush exercises, to name but a few." He directed his attention at Connor. "Alpha team has already completed the introductory lessons, so you've got a lot of catching up to do. But your martial arts experience should help."

Draining his coffee mug, the colonel switched off the projector and gathered his papers together. "I'll see everyone after break for our next session."

Alpha team rose in respect as the colonel departed the briefing room.

Connor shut down his laptop with relief. "*Phew* . . . There's a lot to take in," he remarked.

"You've barely scratched the surface," replied Marc. "Your brain will be fried by the end of the month."

"That's if he's got a brain," cracked Jason.

"Leave him alone," said Ling. "Just because yours still needs to evolve."

Jason made a grab for her. Ling sidestepped him and danced down the corridor. As the others headed toward Alpha team's common room, Connor hung back. Walking over to Charley, he bent down to pick up her bag.

"I can do that," she said, neatly flipping it onto the back of her wheelchair.

"Sorry—of course you can," replied Connor, feeling awkward at his presumption. He followed her into the corridor.

"Something on your mind?" she asked.

Not knowing how to broach the subject directly, Connor said, "What made you decide to become a guardian?"

Charley laughed. "Colonel Black."

Connor gave her a puzzled look.

"You've experienced his recruitment methods," she explained. "He's not a man who expects no for an answer."

"But you still had a choice."

Charley nodded. "And I jumped at the chance."

"But why?"

Charley sighed. "A friend of mine was kidnapped. She was never seen again. I've always thought that if I'd known how to protect her, I could have saved her."

"But what do your parents think about you doing this?"

"They died in a plane crash three years ago."

Connor felt his heart go out to her. "I'm sorry to hear that."

"It's all right," she replied, her voice flat and unemotional. "I've sort of come to terms with it now."

But Connor recognized the brave face she put on as the same one he used when someone asked about his dad. She couldn't conceal the deeper grain of sadness in her eyes. "I understand how you feel. I've lost my father too."

Charley stopped and turned to him. Although she said nothing, her tender look of compassion said it all. And as though he'd glimpsed a shooting star, Connor felt a deep connection pass between them.

Breaking away from each other's gaze, they continued through the entrance hall in silence. As they neared the bay window, a shaft of sunlight glinted off the badge on Charley's blouse. In an attempt to change the topic, Connor asked, "Tell me, why's your shield gold?"

Charley glanced down at the badge. "These are awarded for outstanding bravery in the line of duty."

Intrigued, Connor asked, "What did you do?"

Charley rolled to a stop by the window and looked out at the mountains in the distance.

"As guardians, we hope for the best but plan for the worst," she said softly. "Sometimes, the worst happens."

She chewed her lower lip pensively and went silent on him.

Wishing he'd kept his mouth shut, Connor decided not to push the subject any further. Charley seemed to appreciate this. She forced a smile, and her face brightened. "But don't worry, Connor. As ops leader, I'll make certain that never happens to you."

12

Descending the darkened staircase to the basement level, Hazim walked along a short corridor, lit only by a bare bulb, and looked inside an empty, windowless white-walled cell. In the room opposite, Bahir glanced up from a circuit board he was soldering.

"Malik's asked me to check on the progress of the holding cell," explained Hazim. "He wants to know if it'll be one hundred percent secure."

"When I'm finished," Bahir said, the glowing tip of the soldering iron reflecting in his metal-rimmed glasses, "a spider won't be able to get in or out."

He pointed to the narrow door Hazim had just peered through. "That's the only access, and it has a reinforced lock."

"What about electronic communications?"

Bahir indicated a smartphone on his desk. "See for yourself: no signal whatsoever."

Hazim glanced at the display—the aerial icon flashed *Searching.*

"I've installed a wide range of electronic jammers," Bahir quietly boasted, nodding toward his spaghetti junction of wires and boxes on the table. "All operating on different bandwidths. Each jammer has a backup in case of failure. The system will block against every cellular network—even the newer phones that hop between different frequencies."

Hazim nodded, as if understanding the complex array of technical equipment before him. "What about bugs and transmitters?"

Bahir snorted in disdain. "Useless. *All* radio signals are disrupted." He gave an oily smile. "I've employed subtle jamming too. No distortion or erratic tones—that would be too easy to detect. Instead, any listener will just hear silence, although everything will seem superficially normal with their equipment."

"That's pretty impressive," said Hazim.

"Of course it is," said Bahir, returning to his work with a grin.

Hazim coughed politely for Bahir's attention. "Malik's also concerned about thermal-imaging scanners. What should I tell him?"

Without looking up, Bahir pointed to the ceiling and walls. "A combination of aluminum layers and Plexiglas in the construction will foil any attempts to scan this room for body heat—even if there was a full-blown fire, they couldn't detect it."

"Right," said Hazim. "And what about *our* communications?"

Putting down the soldering iron, Bahir took off his glasses and rubbed the bridge of his nose, clearly irritated at being interrupted yet again. "The reach of the jammers is about nine meters, so we'll still be able to operate outside this zone. For Internet access, I've piggybacked the neighboring property's telephone line and installed a rerouter."

"Isn't that risky?" gasped Hazim. "Won't it reveal our location?"

Bahir gave him a hard stare as if insulted by the mere suggestion. "Not at all. The connection is bounced between a dozen random servers worldwide, plus it's protected by a few tricks of my own. There'll be no way they can trace the signal back here."

"And you're *absolutely* certain this room is soundproof?" Hazim asked.

"On my life. Now let me get on with my work," replied Bahir, replacing his glasses and picking up the soldering iron. "For all intents and purposes, this room is invisible to the eyes and ears of the US government. In essence, it does not exist."

13

Marc had been right. After a couple of weeks, Connor's brain was turning to mush. He had never imagined he would need to know so much to become a bodyguard. There had been lectures on the law—common, civil and criminal. How to produce a threat assessment. The basics of operational planning. Conflict management. Etiquette at formal functions. And even how to get safely in and out of a car: sit backside first, instead of stepping in with one foot. Then if the car sped away in an emergency, you simply lifted your legs— rather than being dumped unceremoniously on the pavement as the vehicle shot off without you.

And this was just the start. He still had ten weeks of *basic* training ahead. On top of that, they were expected to attend normal classes—math, history, English and all the other subjects Connor had hoped to escape by joining Guardian. But Colonel Black took all aspects of his recruits' training seriously. "In all but the most extreme circumstances, a professional bodyguard uses brain over brawn," he explained. "And that means being educated and informed."

After another marathon day of nonstop classes and fitness training, Connor collapsed on the sofa in Alpha team's common room. "When will we get some time off?" he asked.

Ling, helping herself to a Diet Coke from the fridge, merely laughed. "You mean, for good behavior? We might have a trip to Cardiff every so often. But don't get your hopes up. This course is full-on."

She pointed to the next week's schedule pinned on the bulletin board. "Read it and weep!"

Dragging himself from the sofa, Connor passed Amir, who was busily tapping away on his keyboard. "Don't you ever stop working?"

"This isn't work; it's programming," explained Amir, his eyes fixated on the screen. "I'm creating a bodyguard app."

"What will it do?" asked Connor, trying to get a look.

Amir tapped the side of his nose with a finger to indicate a secret. "I'll tell you when it works."

"Sounds intriguing."

"Don't get too excited," Ling said, smirking. "Amir's last app fried his phone."

Amir raised his nose at her. "The phone just couldn't handle the sheer awesomeness of my programming, that's all."

"Whatever," said Ling, sipping her can of Coke and strolling out.

Connor scanned the schedule. He groaned when he saw he had a double period of math first thing Monday morning. His eyes skipped over the standard subjects to the bodyguard lessons—which, truth be told, fascinated him. Even if they were demanding and pushing him to his limit, he realized this was the sort of training his father must have had.

Foot drills. World affairs. Hostage survival. Route planning. Embus and debus training. Vehicle searches. Unarmed combat—

A relieved smile broke across Connor's face. At least he'd be one step ahead of the others in that class.

14

Connor entered the gym with Charley and the rest of Alpha team. A group of kids hung around the basketball court. When they spotted Charley, they strolled over.

"Aren't you that surfer girl?" asked a young lad with wavy brown hair. "Charley Hunter?"

Charley nodded.

"Wow!" he said, eyes widening in starstruck glee. He turned to his friends. "I told you so. This girl was the Quiksilver Junior Surfing Champion. She conquered the Banzai Pipeline in Hawaii."

The kids began to crowd around her wheelchair. One of the girls produced a pen and asked for an autograph. Worried that Charley was going to be mobbed, Connor stepped forward.

"Hey, watch it!" snarled a boy dressed in combats and a death-metal T-shirt, his way blocked by Connor.

"Sorry, mate, but you need to give her some space."

"I just wanted to get her autograph," mumbled the boy, moodily stuffing his hands in his pockets.

Suddenly Connor caught sight of a blade. "KNIFE!" he shouted as the boy thrust for Charley.

Relying on his jujitsu training, Connor grabbed the boy's wrist. He was almost too late, the tip of the blade sweeping a hair's breadth from Charley's throat. The other kids scattered in panic as the two of them fought for control over the lethal weapon. Connor twisted the boy's arm using the *kote-gaeshi* technique to drive him to the floor. The boy still refused to let go of the knife. Jason dived on top, pinning the attacker to the ground, while Ling and Amir rushed Charley toward the exit.

A man clapped for them to stop.

"Excellent reactions," commended Steve, their unarmed combat instructor. Ex–British Special Forces, he was a six-foot-two man-mountain with skin as dark as ebony and the muscles of a gladiator. He'd also been the other phony police officer involved in Connor's recruitment. "That training exercise demonstrates how difficult it is to foresee an attack. But you handled it well. The Principal was saved."

He glanced at the red ink line marking Connor's left forearm where the rubber knife had caught him.

"You, on the other hand, are seriously injured."

Connor grimaced, disappointed with himself for not managing to cleanly disarm the attacker from Delta team.

"Knife attacks are possibly the most dangerous of all close-quarter combat situations. That's why the best way to tackle a threat is not to tackle it at all," Steve explained as he collected the training weapon. "Avoidance and escape should always be your first priority as a bodyguard. This is *not* cowardice. Remember, it's far better to make a good run than a bad stand."

He beckoned for Alpha and Delta teams to gather around.

"However, there will be times when escape is impossible and you must take the threat head-on to defend yourself and your Principal. If you're forced to fight, end it fast. It should be over within five to ten seconds. A punch to the face. A knife-hand strike to the throat. A kick to the groin. Whatever it takes."

Steve slammed a meaty fist into the palm of his hand for emphasis. The class all nodded obediently. They'd spent the first hour of the lesson doing pad work. Drilling jabs, crosses, front kicks and roundhouses over and over to commit them to muscle memory—so that the techniques became instinctive rather than reactive. For Connor, this was already the case. So, while many of the other recruits struggled to master the moves, he relished getting his teeth back into his martial arts training.

"But remember the whole purpose of any defensive action is to escape with your Principal," continued their instructor.

"You're hitting to buy time. Even in the middle of a conflict you should be looking for the way out."

He pointed to the green emergency exit sign by way of example.

"But you can't go around punching and kicking every potential threat. First, the person could be innocent with no intention of harming your Principal. Second, you'll end up in court for assault. That's why it's useful to have several nonlethal techniques in your armory. Ling and Connor, because you're both black belts, I need you to demonstrate."

They stepped forward. Steve instructed Ling to hold her arm out straight. Then he positioned her middle finger on the bone of Connor's sternum just above his solar plexus.

"Connor, walk toward Ling."

Since Ling was small and willowy, Connor saw no problem in getting past her. But as soon as he stepped forward, there was a sharp pain in his chest.

"Come on!" chided Steve. "You're a strong lad. It shouldn't be too difficult."

Connor pushed harder, but the pain only increased. And Ling wasn't even straining as she held him back.

His combat instructor seemed to enjoy the astonished look on his face.

"That's how you keep someone at bay with *just a finger*."

15

"The single-finger technique's effective only if the person is a mere annoyance to your Principal," explained Steve. "But if they're determined and becoming a serious threat, you may need to be more *insistent* and use a different PAL technique."

"PAL?" asked Connor, having never heard of such a martial art style.

"Pain-assisted learning," replied his instructor with a wicked grin.

Asking Ling to step aside, he stood in front of Connor. Holding out a muscular arm, he gently fended Connor off with his fingertips.

"Have you heard of Bruce Lee's one-inch punch?"

Connor nodded.

"Well, this is the one-inch push."

With barely more than a flick of his wrist, Steve palmed Connor in the chest. Taken completely by surprise, Connor staggered backward and then collapsed to the floor, gasping for breath. A concussive wave of pain spread through his lungs, and his chest felt as if it had imploded.

"Effective, isn't it?" commented Steve, helping him back to his feet.

Rubbing his chest, Connor managed a small grunt of acknowledgment. These skills were on a totally different level from his kickboxing and jujitsu training.

While Connor recovered, Steve explained the workings of the technique. "Like a coiled-up spring, you drive your body weight through your arm and into the person's chest. This move can be as powerful as a punch, but you appear to be doing hardly anything. So, if your victim complains, what are they going to say?" Steve put on a whiny, petulant voice. *"He pushed me, Officer!"*

The class laughed. Then, putting on chest pads, they began practicing the two techniques on one another. Connor was partnered with Jason.

"That looked like it really *hurt*," said Jason with the trace of a smile.

"Felt like he cracked a rib," Connor replied, still rubbing his chest.

"Well, I'd better let you go first, then. Give you time to recover."

Connor got the distinct impression that Jason was implying he was weak rather than making the offer out of any friendly concern. *Just you wait*, Connor thought, holding out his arm to fend off his partner.

Jason strode forward, seemingly utterly confident of over-powering Connor. Then he grimaced in pain and frustration as he failed to push past Connor's finger.

"So it really *does* work!" he exclaimed.

"Oh yes, but not as much as this," replied Connor, copying his instructor's movements for the second attack. Letting his arm flex like a spitting cobra, he one-inch-pushed Jason in the chest.

Even with the protective pad, Jason grunted in shock and doubled over.

"I see . . . what you mean," he groaned.

"Sorry," said Connor, surprising even himself with the force of the strike.

"Don't worry . . . mate," said Jason, standing upright. "Now it's *my* turn!"

Jason didn't bother with the single-finger technique. He went straight to the one-inch push. Connor flew backward, barreling into two students from Delta team.

"I *like* this attack," said Jason, cracking his knuckles. "Move over, Bruce Lee!"

Apologizing to the two recruits, Connor returned to face his partner. Although his chest throbbed madly, he tried not to show any pain.

"Not bad," he wheezed—then one-inch-pushed Jason.

Jason fell flat on the floor. Gasping for breath, his face contorted in fury, he leaped to his feet and immediately took his turn, striking even harder this time. They continued to exchange pushes, their chests becoming more bruised and battered with every attempt to outdo each other. Then, without warning, their training suddenly escalated into a full-blown fight, and Connor found himself tussling with Jason on the gym floor.

Two meaty hands seized them by the scruffs of their necks and pulled them apart. Their instructor lifted them off the ground until they were at his eye level.

"Anger is only one letter away from danger," Steve warned them sternly. "Control your anger. Otherwise anger will control you and you'll lose focus. As a guardian, you want to fight smarter, not harder. Do you two understand?"

Chastened, Connor and Jason nodded in response.

"Good. Now shake up and make up," Steve ordered.

Still dangling off the floor, Connor offered his hand to Jason. He had no idea who'd started the fight, but he knew the last thing he needed was an enemy on the team. "Sorry. Looks like we got a bit carried away."

After a moment's hesitation the other boy shook it. "No worries. At least we've battle-tested the technique!" he said, grinning.

With the apologies made, their instructor seemed satisfied and dropped them both to the ground.

"Well, now you've *mastered* the one-inch push," he mocked. "We'll finish with one last technique—the head twist."

This time Steve selected a tall boy from Delta team for his demonstration.

"Again, there is very little to this defensive attack. That's what makes it effective. Lift the chin, twist the head and simply push down."

Steve grabbed the boy's jaw and, in an effortless push and twist, made the boy collapse like a concertina.

"Basically, where the head goes, the body follows," he explained.

Connor was impressed—the move used the same principles as jujitsu in exploiting the weaknesses of the human body. With it, he should be able to take anyone down in a few seconds.

"That's fine if you're similar heights. But how's Charley going to manage that one?" questioned Amir, referring to her using a wheelchair.

Before Steve could answer, Charley rolled her chair over Amir's toes. He squealed in pain. She punched him in the stomach and he doubled over. Then she grabbed his head and twisted him to the ground.

"Very easily," replied Charley as Amir lay bowed and defeated at her feet.

16

Connor looked into the athletic wear store window on the second floor of Cardiff's Queens Arcade. He barely noticed the display of Nike sneakers on sale. Instead, his eyes were focused on the reflection in the glass. A steady stream of people was passing behind him. Most, if not all, were innocent shoppers. But among that Saturday crowd *someone* was following him. He didn't know who yet, but he was determined to find out.

Walking on, Connor headed down the escalator to the ground level of the shopping center. He crossed the polished tiled floor and stopped beside the information sign. Pretending to be lost, he examined the map, then casually glanced around. As his eyes swept the atrium, he scanned the faces of the people descending the escalator: a blond-haired woman in a green jacket . . . a harassed-looking mother clasping her toddler's hand . . . two teenage girls plastered with eyeliner and lipstick . . . a man on his phone—

Hadn't he seen that face before?

The square jaw. The broad nose. The deep-set eyes. Although Connor couldn't be certain, he thought he'd noticed the man earlier while browsing in the video-game store.

Connor decided not to hang around. He headed along the central concourse toward the south exit. All the while he kept his eye on reflections in the plate-glass windows. Twice he caught glimpses of the square-jawed man. But was the man actually following him or just innocently leaving by the same route?

To test his hunch, Connor stopped outside a fashion store. After a few paces, the man paused at a newsstand and began studying the papers. Connor felt his pulse quicken. This could be pure coincidence still, but the man's behavior seemed increasingly suspicious. He was leafing through the newspapers without really looking at them. At the same time he was mumbling to himself—*or perhaps into a concealed radio?*

Connor now needed to prove beyond a doubt that this individual was on his tail. But he didn't want to alert the man that he suspected anything. That would scare him off—and then Connor might never find out who this person was or why he was following him. He glimpsed a gold stud in the man's right ear and made a mental note of it. Then he headed for the exit.

When he reached the glass doors, he held them open to

let a woman with a stroller through, and took the opportunity to subtly check behind him.

The concourse was busy with shoppers. But the man was nowhere in sight.

Maybe all this bodyguard training is making me paranoid? Connor thought.

Stepping outside into the bright spring sunshine, he turned right to weave between the hordes of people milling along Queen Street. The air was filled with the shouts of street hawkers and the strumming of street musicians. A local bus roared by, sending up a cloud of diesel fumes.

Connor glanced at the time on his phone. He had five minutes before he was due to meet the others. Heading along the road, he couldn't shake off the feeling that he was still being watched—though he realized that if anyone was following him now, it would be almost impossible to spot them among the crowds. What he needed was a quieter yet public area to draw the individual out into the open.

Up ahead, a blue sign pointed toward a parking garage. Perfect.

Connor checked for traffic, then crossed the road. As he reached the opposite curb, he heard the blast of a car horn. Glancing over his shoulder, he saw the square-jawed man had narrowly missed being run over. Although Connor's gaze was directly upon him, the man deliberately avoided eye contact by staring at a blond-haired woman in a red jacket and sunglasses standing at a bus stop. But Connor wasn't fooled. This man was after him.

Quickening his pace, Connor turned right through a pedestrian walkway to the parking lot. His tail would have to follow him through the narrow alley—and if he did, Connor's suspicions would be confirmed.

He was halfway across the parking lot, and still the man hadn't appeared. Just as he thought he'd lost him, Connor spied the man standing by the ticket machine at the lot's main entrance. Clearly out of breath from running, the man was pretending to look in his pockets for change. While he was distracted, Connor whipped out his phone and took a picture of him. With the evidence in his pocket, Connor ducked behind a van, intending to escape and return to the others. But a stocky man with a head as bald as a bowling ball stepped out and confronted him.

17

The man was chewing slowly on a stick of gum as he blocked Connor's way.

"Did you get a good shot?" he asked.

"Yes," replied Connor, showing his phone to his surveillance tutor. "It was the square-jawed man with the gold stud in his right ear."

Bugsy raised an eyebrow, mildly impressed. "And what about the woman who was following you? Did you take a photo of her too?"

Connor's brow creased in puzzlement. "What woman?"

"The blonde in the green jacket."

Connor vaguely remembered someone fitting that description, but couldn't quite place where he'd seen her.

"What about the one in the red jacket and sunglasses?" asked Bugsy.

"You mean the woman by the bus stop?"

Bugsy nodded.

"No," admitted Connor. "That was the first time I'd seen her."

"They're the same person," revealed his surveillance tutor with a grin. "Just a reversible coat and sunglasses. It's amazing how a simple disguise can be enough to fool the untrained observer. And a word of warning: women are far better chameleons than men in that regard."

Charley and the rest of Alpha team appeared from behind the van.

"So how did Connor fare at anti-surveillance?" Bugsy asked them.

"Pretty good. For a first attempt," said Amir, punching Connor lightly on the arm.

"He kept his techniques covert," observed Marc. "Nice use of windows and natural looking around."

Connor smiled, pleased by his friends' compliments.

"Until he stared right at his tail in the main street, that is," Jason was keen to point out. "That was overt. The guy knew he was onto him then."

Connor hadn't expected praise from Jason—and didn't get any. Their relationship was still pretty frosty after their unarmed combat tussle the week before.

"But loads of people looked," argued Ling. "That idiot almost got himself killed."

"I think Connor was clever to use the alley as a 'choke point,'" noted Charley.

"Agreed," said Bugsy. "If any tail had followed him through, their surveillance would have been exposed. But he still failed to spot the woman."

He pointed to a blue estate car two rows behind Connor. The blond-haired woman was behind the wheel. She gave Connor a teasing wave. Beside her sat the square-jawed man with the gold stud.

"You must remember that experienced operatives work in teams. There won't be just one person following you or your Principal. And they'll take turns to avoid detection."

Connor nodded, his lesson learned. Bugsy had been training Alpha team in anti-surveillance techniques for the past week. He'd explained that any coordinated attack was always preceded by a period of surveillance. If that surveillance was detected early enough, the attack might be abandoned. The problem was spotting the operatives in the first place. And if the enemy was an organized terrorist group, then they would be highly trained and virtually impossible to detect.

"Criminals, terrorists and kidnappers look the same as everyone else," Bugsy reminded them. "Men, women, young and old, any could be monitoring your Principal. Children—just like *you*—are also used as information gatherers. A skilled operative will be the 'gray' person, the one who blends into a crowd—so you have to suspect everyone."

He popped another stick of chewing gum into his mouth before offering the packet around.

"The key to identifying surveillance is to force multiple sightings and unnatural behavior," he explained, chewing voraciously. "Drop a piece of paper and see if anyone picks it up to examine it. Frequently change direction—although try to have a reason for doing that, because otherwise the technique is quite obvious. Get on a bus and jump off at the next stop."

"You could use your smartphone to scan the area for Bluetooth devices," suggested Amir. "If the same username pops up in two or more locations, then you've got a ping."

Bugsy grinned as he chewed. "Now *that's* a new trick!" he remarked, nodding appreciatively at his student. "In terms of unnatural behavior, look for people peering around corners, over stands or through doors and windows. Check for 'mirroring'—if you cross the road, who else crosses the road? They'll have some means of communication, so watch out for a clenched fist or mic switch. A vacant expression on a person can be a dead giveaway—they're concentrating on a radio transmission. Fidgeting, talking to themselves or the avoidance of eye contact are all possible signs. Also be vigilant for handovers. If you suspect an individual, watch them closely but covertly. They may identify another operative by hand signals, eye contact or using a cell phone."

Connor now realized that the square-jawed man's stare

at the blond-haired woman had been a blatant signal—and he'd missed it.

"Anti-surveillance is sometimes the only way to meet a threat and deter—or even survive—an attack," Bugsy emphasized. "So stay in Code Yellow and keep your eyes peeled for repeated sightings. Remember: Once is happenstance. Twice is circumstance. Three times means enemy action."

18

Hazim kept the submachine gun tucked into his shoulder as he crouched behind the rusting oil barrel. A soldier with a rifle emerged from behind a building to his left. Hazim squeezed the trigger. His weapon let loose a deafening barrage. The soldier was hit in quick succession by four body shots.

Almost immediately two more soldiers appeared. Kedar, who stood in the shelter of a nearby doorway, raked them with gunfire. Then a woman darted across from the opposite building. Hazim targeted her, but his initial burst of bullets missed. Hurriedly re-aiming, he fired again. The woman was winged twice in the hip before going down.

More enemies popped up. Hazim sprayed them in a deadly hail of gunfire, the submachine gun jarring against his shoulder like a jackhammer. His palms became sticky with sweat, and a red haze seized him as the gun thundered in his grip. He spun on a girl standing in a doorway.

His bullets ripped through her too. Only too late did he realize his mistake as the teddy bear clasped in her arms was shredded into tatters.

"Cease fire!" barked Kedar.

Hazim took a trembling finger off the trigger. His breathing was rapid, and the air was tainted with the smell of burned gunpowder and hot metal.

"Good shooting," commended Kedar, slapping Hazim on the back.

"I'm sorry—I didn't mean to kill the girl," replied Hazim. "I lost control."

Kedar grinned. "It's easily done. With one of those guns in your hand, you can feel invincible. But you must remain focused."

Kedar reset the cardboard targets on the private shooting range and turned to the other men in the group.

"The Secret Service agents will be well armed and highly trained," he warned them. "That's why we must be capable of holding our own in a gun battle."

He raised his compact submachine gun aloft. "But don't worry, we'll possess equal firepower and meet force with force."

Kedar aimed at the farthest target on the range and planted a bullet straight between the figure's eyes, before obliterating the target's head.

19

The *crack* of a gunshot shattered the peace of the valley, sending a flock of startled birds into the sky.

"RUN!" bawled Amir into Connor's ear.

Roughly seized by the shoulder, Connor was spun around and shoved in the direction opposite of the shooter. Amir was directly behind him, holding his body close to shield Connor from the threat. Like some mad three-legged race, they sprinted across the field for the safety of a stone wall.

"Keep going," ordered Amir, gripping him tightly.

As they neared the wall, Connor spotted a burning fuse amid the grass.

"Grenade!" he cried.

Amir's eyes widened in panic and he attempted to alter their course. But their feet became tangled up by the sudden change in direction. They both tumbled to the ground, landing face-first in the dirt. The grenade exploded inches from their heads. There was a blinding flash. An earsplitting blast. Then a shower of red sparks rained down on them.

"That was close," remarked Amir, laughing nervously as the firecracker burned out.

Connor dislodged Amir from his back and glared at him. "Not as close as this sheep muck!"

Amir stifled a snigger as Connor wiped off a dark brown smear of dung from his face with his sleeve.

"Gross," said Amir, but his amusement was brought to a swift end when he heard the angry shouts of their instructor.

"A-C-E," said Jody despairingly as the two of them rejoined Alpha team on the school's front lawn. "Amir, have you forgotten what that means?"

Amir shook his head. "Assess the threat. Counter the danger. Escape the kill zone."

"Then why didn't you assess your escape route? It's no good running with your Principal if you're heading in the wrong direction. Or worse—toward the threat itself!"

Jody was teaching Alpha team the concept of "body cover": how to effectively shield a Principal from an attack. They'd spent all day doing "action-on drills": grabbing their Principal from sitting, standing, walking and running positions, and covering them against various assaults from the front, rear, left, right, and even from above. Through constant practice, the aim was to make A-C-E as instinctive as ducking.

"Whenever there's an apparent danger, you must assess the situation *before* you react," Jody reminded them. "This might take a millisecond or ten seconds, but it's vital to your survival. The threat—whether it is a punch, a knife, a bullet or even an egg—determines your response. Then, once the assessment is made, you cover your Principal, placing yourself between them and the threat. For example—"

She grabbed Marc, stepped in front of him and shouted, "STAY BEHIND ME!"

The demonstration took less than a second, but was effective.

"You need to control the Principal both physically and verbally," she explained, still holding on to Marc's arm. "The shock of the attack might have caused *fight*, *flight* or *freeze*. This could mean the Principal is either functioning with you or has brain fade. Whatever the case, you need to stay in control and ensure they don't hamper the evacuation." Jody held up her right hand. "Leave your strong arm free to punch and defend. And, when you do evacuate, the body cover must remain on. As you've just witnessed with Connor and Amir's spectacular belly flop into the sheep dung, this isn't easy. Which is why you need to *practice*."

She released Marc and asked Connor to step forward. "Punch Marc," she instructed.

Marc looked shocked. "But he's a kickboxing champion!"

"And I'm your bodyguard," replied Jody with a wink.

Obeying his instructor, Connor swung a fist at Marc's face.

"GET DOWN!" screamed Jody, leaping forward and driving

her hip into Marc. He was shoved so violently sideways that he was thrown several feet. But he was no longer under any direct threat, and Jody now engaged with the attack. Effortlessly blocking it, she countered with a hook punch that stopped just short of Connor's jaw.

"You see, by *suddenly* moving your Principal, the assailant doesn't know where to look: at his original target or at you, his new threat."

Jody lowered her fist and patted Connor on the shoulder. "Remember to block next time," she said with a grin.

"Isn't the technique a bit *aggressive*?" Connor asked as Marc stood, rubbing his bruised hip. "You could hurt the Principal."

"In a life-threatening situation, this technique needs to be aggressive," Jody replied. "The Shove, as I like to call it, will save your Principal from any direct attack—a punch, a knife or even a bullet."

"We're expected to take a *bullet* for someone else?" exclaimed Amir.

Jody's expression became solemn. "Ideally, with your training, it won't ever come to that. And even if it did, you should be wearing your issued body armor. But when you're on assignment, you take on the very same danger your Principal faces. You are their shield. That's why bodyguards are sometimes known as *bullet-catchers*."

20

The waves rolled toward the shore, long white lines that peeled in perfect curls. Bobbing on the sea's surface like eager seals, local surfers waited to catch their ride and follow the surge in. Along the three-mile stretch of golden sand, a few families dotted the shoreline, but otherwise the beach belonged to Alpha team. After twelve weeks of basic training, they'd finally earned some proper time off and Steve had driven them to the Gower Peninsula to relax. Now it was June, and the sun was warm, the sky cloudless and the day perfect for a barbecue on the beach.

Jason prodded the sausages and slapped on a couple more burgers.

"These should be done in a minute," he announced, swigging from a can of Coke.

Ling lay on her beach towel, soaking up the sun's rays. "Did you keep my veggie kebabs separate?"

"Of course," said Jason, quickly shuffling Ling's food to

one side and sharing a guilty grin with Connor and Marc. Now that training was over, the rivalry between them had relaxed a little. Although their relationship was still fractious, Connor had come to realize that Jason wasn't a bad guy. It was just that neither of them wanted to be second best.

For Connor, the past twelve weeks had flown by, and he felt like a completely different person. When a geography lesson was paired with survival in hostage situations, a physics class with fire training, and cross-country running with anti-ambush drills, the mix was mind-blowing. It was as if he now wore special lenses that identified every threat surrounding him on a daily basis. Connor no longer classed this as "paranoia"—he was simply *aware* of the world, living in Code Yellow. When he walked down a busy street, passersby seemed to be in a perpetual, and worrying, state of half sleep. *Did they notice the security camera above the shopping center entrance recording them? Did they have a clue where the fire exit was in an emergency? Had any of them spotted the suspicious individual hanging near the ATM?* As a direct result of his training, Connor instinctively picked up on these details. And though he was alert to more danger, he paradoxically felt safer, since he was now prepared to deal with any trouble that might occur.

Connor wondered if his mum or gran would notice the difference in him when he returned to London for summer

vacation. Despite the intensity of the training, he'd managed to call home every week. His mother always sounded
upbeat and eager to hear news of his progress, although
he could tell by the edge in her voice that she was often
in a great deal of pain. He had to gloss over the details of
his bodyguard training, but she was pleased he was learning new subjects as well as continuing his martial arts. His
gran seemed happy too, and particularly glad he was paying
attention to his "other" studies. Sally was proving a great
help around the house, and she'd taken his mum and gran
to local parks and gardens and on day trips out of London,
something the two of them never could have managed before. Any doubts Connor had about joining Guardian were
dispelled each time he heard about the care they were re-
ceiving. Whatever the commitment in becoming a bodyguard, the sacrifice was worthwhile.

Connor watched a surfer catch a wave and ride it all the
way in.

"So could *you* do it?" asked Amir.

"Surf like that?" said Connor. "No chance."

"I mean"—Amir dug his foot into the sand—"take a bullet
for someone else?"

Connor glanced at his friend. Ever since their body-cover
lesson, the specter of being a "bullet-catcher" had hung
over them. No one really talked about it, but Connor had
thought long and hard about the matter. Was this a risk he

was willing to take? Had his father made such a sacrifice? He'd never been told the full story. And, if his father had, did *he* have the guts to throw himself in the line of fire?

"Perhaps," replied Connor. "If I cared enough about the person."

"But as a guardian you won't know the person at first," said Marc.

"And worse—you might not even like them!" added Jason, flipping a burger and glancing in Connor's direction.

Ling pulled out her headphones. "I wouldn't worry about it, Amir. Jody says such a situation rarely happens."

"Rarely doesn't mean *never*," replied Amir. "And who's to say another person's life is worth more than mine?"

"I suppose it's about standing up for what is right," said Connor. "The strong protecting the weak."

"That's easier said than done," Ling pointed out. "And Charley should know."

Charley had rolled down the beach to the point where the last gush of the waves fingered the shore. The sea rushed around her wheels, and her feet were lost in the swirling white waters.

"Is Charley all right down there?" asked Connor.

Ling glanced from beneath her shades and nodded. "She likes to get close. Reminds her of her competition days."

Connor thought back to their unarmed combat scenario. "So Charley actually *was* a pro surfer?"

Jason laughed. "Do koalas live in trees? Charley was awe-some! Youngest Quiksilver Champion ever."

Connor looked at Charley, constrained by her wheelchair. He could only imagine the frustration she was experiencing at being unable to surf—if he couldn't practice martial arts, he'd go mad. "I'll go tell her the food's ready."

Grabbing a drink from the cooler, he wandered down to the shoreline.

"I thought you might like a Diet Coke," he said, offering Charley the ice-cold can.

She accepted it and offered him a brief smile.

"There's a good swell today," she said wistfully. "Nothing like LA, but the breaks are clean and long."

Connor nodded as if he knew what she was talking about. He wished he had more knowledge of surfer speak. The icy cold sea washed up his legs, soaking his shorts, and he jumped back.

Charley didn't move. "I just love the feel of the waves. Their power. The overwhelming rush as the surf seizes you. Nothing in the world compares to riding a wave."

Connor studied her face, bathed in the golden sun, her bright eyes keenly following a surfer. He noticed that in her hand she clasped the gold Guardian badge.

She's certainly brave, he thought, *but was the sacrifice worth it?*

21

"Mr. President, here are the files on the organization you inquired about."

"Thank you, George," said President Mendez, taking the folder marked Confidential from his White House chief of staff.

Leaning back in his leather chair in the Oval Office, he studied the winged shield on the first page, then read the opening summary. After a thoughtful pause, he glanced over to a broad-chested man dressed in full military attire.

"You can vouch for this Colonel Black, General?"

"One hundred percent, Mr. President," replied General Martin Shaw, chairman of the Joint Chiefs of Staff and the highest-ranking military officer in the United States Armed Forces. "Colonel Black and I go back a long way. Kuwait, Iraq, Afghanistan. I'd trust him with my life."

"What about your child's?" remarked a tall man pointedly, who sat ramrod straight on the Oval Office's cream upholstered couch. With premature gray hair and stress lines around his eyes, Dirk Moran, the director of the Secret Service, was far less enthusiastic about the proposal on the agenda.

The general nodded. "If you met the colonel, you would too."

"But we're not talking about him, are we?" replied Dirk, pushing his objection further. "We're considering a *child* protecting the president's daughter."

"Yes, but they're fully trained in the intricacies of close protection," argued the White House chief of staff. "And this Guardian organization has an impressive track record."

"So does my son on sports day, but I'm not considering him for the Olympics," said Dirk, standing up as he struggled to control his frustration. "A child bodyguard is a joke! Trained or otherwise, they're simply not in the same league as a Secret Service agent."

"That's true. They're in an entirely *different* league," observed the general, raising an eyebrow. "No one would ever suspect a kid of being a bodyguard. A guardian would provide an 'invisible' ring of protection around the president's daughter. He or she can go where your Secret Service agents can't."

Dirk turned to the president, whose dark brown eyes followed their discussion with interest.

"Mr. President, you have at your disposal the finest and

most dedicated close-protection force in the world," he implored. "Are you convinced this is necessary?"

The chief of staff stepped forward and interrupted with a polite cough. "Dirk, you can't deny that there have been a few holes in the Secret Service net recently."

Dirk's jaw tightened. "Granted, but they have been *plugged.*"

"I have complete faith in your team, Dirk," assured President Mendez. "But, considering the severe threat level the director of National Intelligence has advised us of, a guardian seems like a sensible extra precaution."

"I've read Karen Wright's report," Dirk said. "All the more reason to *tighten* security. Not to introduce a weakness. We need only double the Secret Service team."

"You know my daughter won't stand for any increased protection," replied the president, holding his hands up in resigned despair. "That was the source of the problem in the first place."

"We can function *low* profile. There's no need to resource externally—"

"Dirk, I understand your concerns. But I must consider every option when it comes to my family's safety. Let me examine the profiles first. If none prove suitable, we won't pursue the matter any further. Is that acceptable?"

Dirk nodded reluctantly and sat back down.

When it came to serious decisions, President Mendez

always kept his cards close to his chest. Therefore he hadn't disclosed the similar doubts that he shared with his Secret Service director. It seemed unbelievable that he was considering entrusting the life of his daughter into the hands of someone her own age! The guardian in question would have to be truly exceptional to deserve his approval.

He studied each of the profiles in turn, his forefinger rubbing at his temple as he read. The list of potential candidates was short but impressive, their credentials and training equal to any professional close-protection officer.

Dirk watched as the president turned over each page, setting none aside. When the final profile was reached, he allowed himself a satisfied smirk. At last he could put this absurd proposal back into his filing cabinet where it belonged and get on with his job of protecting the president and his family.

"I cannot believe this," uttered President Mendez under his breath.

"I'm glad you agree, Mr. President," said Dirk, shooting a subtle but triumphant glance at his associates. "However, you can be assured that my department will maintain impenetrable security around your daughter."

But President Mendez wasn't listening. He held up the last sheet and handed it to his chief of staff.

"Contact Colonel Black immediately," he instructed. "Tell him that we'll be requiring his organization's services."

Dirk leaped from the sofa to look at the profile in George's grasp. As he scanned the president's choice, his expression crumbled into one of sheer disbelief. "But this guardian hasn't even completed a single assignment yet!"

The president closed the file and replied with complete conviction. "He's the one."

22

Hazim sat alone in the study of the large rented house. The residence had come partly furnished, and he tapped his fingers impatiently on the mahogany desk as he watched the clock on the wall, its second hand ticking by. It was two minutes to seven.

His phone rang, and Hazim snatched it up from the desk. "Hello?"

"Hazim, it's your mother," said the voice at the other end of the line. "Are you still coming over for dinner?"

Sighing, Hazim rubbed his eyes in exhaustion. "Sorry, Mother, I have to work late. Perhaps tomorrow."

He clicked on the eBay home page on his laptop and began browsing the sporting goods section.

"Again?" she protested. "This new job of yours might pay well, but they're overworking you."

"I have to make a good impression."

He glanced up at the clock. It was one minute to seven. Ten seconds to go.

"But I'm worried for your health. It's no good working all hours. You need to rest too—"

"I recently took a vacation," interrupted Hazim, his mouse hovering over the bike category. The minute hand flicked to 19:00.

"Yes, and the family are desperate to know how your trip went. Your sister and brother are missing you. Please come over. Your father will be most disappointed if you don't . . ."

As his mother ranted on, Hazim selected the category filters: *Men's, Mountain Bikes, Used, 20-inch frame, red color*. Five postings were listed. The last of the bikes was in a terrible state, its frame dented and chipped, the front wheel bent, a pedal missing: starting price two hundred dollars. No sane person would bid for such an item. Nonetheless, Hazim clicked on the link, and the image of the bike popped up with a basic description. The auction was set for a day—twenty-three hours and fifty-eight minutes were remaining. But Hazim had no interest in placing a bid.

"Are you still listening to me?"

"Yes, Mother."

"Can you pick up your sister next week?"

"Of course," he replied, groaning as if annoyed by the request, but the corners of his mouth flickered the faintest of smiles.

Using a specialized download helper, Hazim extracted the image of the bike from the browser to his desktop. Then he dropped the file into an application called Scrub. The program opened up automatically and the bike appeared in a fresh window. The image immediately began to disintegrate.

"Hazim, promise to join us for dinner tomorrow," pleaded his mother. "It's the weekend."

"Promise," he replied, and put the phone down.

The decrypting program had finished its work. The mangled bike was replaced by two lines of text that had been digitally embedded within the image:

```
KINGFISHER LANDING 1030, STAFFORD, 3 DAYS.
BEGIN SURVEILLANCE OF EAGLE'S NEST.
```

23

"What's going on?" asked Connor as he hurried down the corridor and caught up with Amir and Marc. He'd been in his room packing to go home for summer vacation when his phone had pinged with a message from Colonel Black:

Alpha team. Briefing room. ASAP.

"Maybe he wants to wish us a happy vacation," suggested Amir.

"If only," replied Marc. "I reckon it's far more serious than that."

Jason and Ling joined them, and they entered the briefing room. Charley was already there, deep in discussion with the colonel. A nervous anticipation gripped Connor when he caught sight of Charley's stunned expression. Whatever the colonel had to say, the news had evidently taken her by surprise.

Hurriedly they found their seats. Colonel Black finished

talking with Charley and turned to them. His face wore a rare smile.

"Alpha team's leave is postponed," he announced, not even bothering to soften the blow.

A groan of disappointment escaped Amir's lips.

The colonel disregarded this and continued, "Guardian has received a top-priority assignment. And a member of *this* team has been selected."

"Who?" asked Ling, perching on the edge of her seat in excitement.

The colonel's steel-gray eyes fell on Connor.

"Me?" said Connor, almost breathless. As the realization sank in, he was unsure whether to be thrilled or terrified at the prospect of his first assignment.

"Yeah, why Connor? He's the newbie," argued Jason, puffing up his chest. "Next to Charley, I'm the most experienced. It should be me."

"I admire your eagerness, Jason," replied Colonel Black tactfully. "But, as with every assignment, it's not simply about an operation being available; it's about the guardian fitting the operation. This assignment is by order of the president of the United States. He chose Connor personally."

Connor was speechless. Surely he'd misunderstood. "He chose me *specifically*. Why?"

"That information wasn't disclosed," replied the colonel.

"It'll be up to President Mendez to reveal his reasons, if he so wishes."

"It's probably because of your martial arts credentials," Charley suggested.

"Well, it certainly can't be for anything else!" mumbled Jason.

Connor let the comment pass, understanding that Jason was crestfallen at not being chosen himself.

"So who's Connor protecting?" asked Marc.

The colonel looked to Charley to respond.

"Alicia Rosa Mendez," she revealed. "The president's daughter."

Marc whistled through his teeth in awe. "Better you than me, Connor."

"Yeah," agreed Ling. "You're going in at the deep end!"

Connor thought there had to be some sort of mistake. "They're right, Colonel. I haven't even done a test operation yet."

The colonel looked him in the eye. "I won't lie to you, Connor. This is the highest-profile assignment Guardian has ever been involved in. For us, we're taking a huge gamble. For you, it will be a baptism of fire. But I've watched your progress closely. You possess your father's ability to think on your feet—and, with any luck, his sixth sense to foresee danger too."

Connor was taken aback by the unexpected comparison

to his father. Their course had been so full-on, he'd not had the opportunity to talk with the colonel about his father's past life. But clearly Colonel Black had been noting the similarities. It was a boost to his confidence, but Connor couldn't help feeling a new pressure on his shoulders of having to live up to the colonel's high expectations.

"Operation Hidden Shield will commence forthwith," declared Colonel Black. "Charley, I want a full profile on the Principal by 0900 hours tomorrow. Amir, prep a go-bag with all the appropriate tactical items. Ling, Marc and Jason, you're responsible for compiling the operation folder. I want maps of all primary locations, threat assessments, sit reps on known hostiles, key personnel and any other relevant information that might help Connor in his task. Connor, come with me for further briefing."

For a moment, Alpha team sat stock-still in their chairs, caught like rabbits in the headlights.

"What are you waiting for?" barked the colonel. "You have your orders."

At his command, they rushed to their stations in the briefing room. Alpha team had run through operational planning situations in training on countless occasions. But this time there was an urgency to their actions. This time it was for real.

24

Connor hardly slept all night. *What reason could one of the most powerful leaders in the world have for selecting me to protect his daughter?*

His martial arts skills couldn't be the only justification. Jason was an equal match to him—in fact, Connor had learned that his rival had once been the Australian Junior Champion. There had to be another reason. But Connor couldn't think what it was. Aside from his twelve weeks of training, he had no real-world experience of being a bodyguard, which worried him deeply. Connor wondered if it was a case of mistaken identity and the president actually believed he was choosing *someone else*.

But the colonel assured him that there'd been no mistake. He was to work alongside the US Secret Service, the Homeland Security department responsible for the protection of the first family. He would be reporting directly to its head, Dirk Moran, while maintaining a line of communication with the Guardian organization in the United Kingdom in case he needed additional support. His mission was to ensure the safety of the president's daughter at all times, particularly in those instances when Secret Service agents couldn't be immediately at hand. The threat level for the operation was deemed Category 1: Life-Threatening.

Connor's mind whirled with the possibilities—angry mobs, long-range snipers, knife-wielding assassins, exploding car bombs . . . The danger list went on and on. And *he* was to be the hidden shield between those threats and the life of the president's daughter. The sheer scale of the task ahead was almost paralyzing. He wondered if his father had ever felt like this before any of his assignments. Or did seasoned bodyguards get used to the pressure? Perhaps it was like a constant trickle of electricity running through their veins, so they felt, yet suppressed, their fears.

And Connor's greatest fear was that he would fail. That at the moment of an attack he would react too late—or, worse still, not react at all.

25

At 9:00, Connor, bleary-eyed and groggy from lack of sleep, joined Alpha team in the briefing room. The other members looked equally exhausted from their late-night research.

"As you know, your Principal is Alicia Rosa Mendez," said Charley, beginning her presentation as soon as Connor was seated. She clicked a remote to display the photo of a young girl on the overhead screen. "Of Mexican-American descent, she is the only daughter of Emilia and Antonio Mendez, the current president of the United States."

Connor studied the photo. Alicia had chocolate-brown eyes, a butter-wouldn't-melt-in-her-mouth smile and a mass of dark curly hair that fell past her shoulders. She looked like any other person his age. It was hard to imagine her as a target for assassins and kidnappers. But that's exactly what she was.

"According to my research and press reports, Alicia is fun-loving and headstrong, and possesses an impulsive streak.

She has slipped her Secret Service protection on several occasions. And, as I understand from the colonel, that is the main reason the president has requested a guardian."

Colonel Black nodded in confirmation. "It's your job, Connor, to stick to her like glue."

Connor briefly wondered how he'd manage that without becoming an annoying hanger-on.

"Alicia attends Montarose School in Washington, DC, where you're now enrolled on a student exchange program for the last two weeks of the semester," Charley explained. "Her grades are good, if not outstanding. Favorite subjects appear to be art, photography and dance. She's in good shape—"

"Most definitely," said Marc with a rakish grin.

"I mean healthy," corrected Charley, shooting him a glare. "Alicia enjoys track and field, and is the captain of the school team. She holds the fastest time for the four hundred meters. So, Connor, you'll be thankful for all those early-morning runs."

Connor and Marc exchanged sideways glances and smirked at each other. Marc had found a shortcut on Alpha team's running route, knocking a good couple of miles off the training. Connor now wished he'd done the full circuit. He was going to suffer for it if he had to keep up with his Principal.

Charley clicked to a new slide titled "Medical History."

"Known medical issues include mild allergies and a history of childhood epilepsy."

"Does that mean she might have a fit?" asked Connor, concerned.

Charley gave a noncommittal shrug. "According to the doctor's reports, her epilepsy seems to have stopped naturally in the last year or so. But it's still something to be aware of. Factors like emotional stress, sleep deprivation and flashing lights have the potential to trigger a seizure."

"I've put some information on epilepsy in the operation folder," Ling interrupted, handing Connor a small USB drive. "There's an action-on sheet explaining how to handle a seizure."

"Thanks," replied Connor, plugging the drive into his laptop.

"The files are all encrypted," she explained, "and accessed by fingerprint recognition." She pointed to the thumb-sized scanner built into the body of his laptop. "I've already programmed it to accept yours. There are also files on Washington, DC, Montarose School, and the White House staff you'll meet, and a hot list identifying the potential threats she faces."

"It's a *long* list," said Jason, yawning widely. "I should know. I was working on it right through the night."

"Perhaps then you'll give Connor a summary of the key groups that pose a risk," suggested Charley.

"Sure," he replied, getting up from his seat and joining her at the front. He took a deep breath and offered Connor a pitying look. "Well, the leader of the free world certainly has some enemies, and Alicia, as his daughter, faces the same dangers. The problems in Yemen, Afghanistan and Pakistan mean that fundamentalists are a major threat. Al-Qaeda and the Taliban are just two of the extremist groups who have the United States and its president in their sights. But it's unlikely they'll target our Principal directly, since their usual methods of attack are bombings, sabotage and scare tactics. Then closer to home, but no less fanatical, are the white supremacists, who dislike having a Latino man as president. They're a real and present danger. Next, we've got the potential for stalkers and lone-wolf assassins—these are almost impossible to identify before they strike, and you'll have to rely on Secret Service intelligence. And, finally, there are the mentally ill, who according to the Secret Service, account for three-quarters of known threats made against the president and his family."

Jason put on a cheery smile for Connor, whose expression had dropped at the seemingly endless list of threats.

"So to put it simply, mate, the world's your enemy."

26

"Here's your go-bag," said Amir, dumping a sleek charcoal-colored backpack on the table. "It contains all you need to run this operation effectively."

He pulled out a super-slim phone from the front pocket.

"Next-generation smartphone," he said, admiring its sleek, elegant form. "Bugsy enhanced this specifically for your assignment. First, fingerprint identification to protect access." He pressed his thumb to the screen, the phone came to life and the Guardian's gleaming winged shield rotated in 3-D on the retina display. "I'm currently programmed in, as are you. But the operating system is firewalled, and any critical breach of it will wipe the hard drive. But don't worry—all stored data is wirelessly backed up to our servers."

His index finger selected an app in the top corner. A crystal-clear bird's-eye view of the Welsh mountains appeared, a small green dot pulsing inside a building that Connor recognized as Guardian headquarters.

"Advanced Mapping app, accurate to the meter with pin-point GPS," explained Amir. "In addition, all the Washington maps are preloaded, plus internal layouts for key buildings such as the White House—at least, those we've got access to—the National Air and Space Museum and the Kennedy Center. Whatever happens, you won't get lost. Nor will your Principal."

He passed Connor a stylish red Armani-branded phone case with a butterfly logo.

"Thanks, but it's a bit girly for me," said Connor, handing it back.

"The case isn't for you," Amir replied. "It's your gift to Alicia and contains a miniature homing beacon. The encoded signal is linked to this Tracker app." He touched a green target icon on the smartphone's screen. The map reappeared, now overlaid with a grid and a flashing red dot beside the blue. "It'll locate the case anywhere within fifteen kilometers and calculate the quickest route from your position. Bugsy recommends that you keep this feature secret—it's for emergency use only."

Amir held up the phone and pointed to the tiny lens on the back. "Ten-megapixel camera with optical zoom, high-definition video, night-vision and instant-face-recognition software. Film or photograph a crowd and it'll ping an individual that it's seen before at a different location. If it records multiple occurrences, the app will highlight the suspected

CHRIS BRADFORD

face in red. But Bugsy says *not* to rely on this app. The Mark
One eyeball is always your best piece of surveillance gear."

Amir winked and Connor laughed. Bugsy often referred
to his eyes as "Mark One."

Opening a small fabric pouch, Amir handed Connor a
tiny flesh-colored earpiece.

"For when you want to communicate covertly," he explained. "It has a vibrational mic that will pick up your voice.
The smartphone acts as your transceiver. Just remember,
the battery life of the earpiece is limited. Eight hours tops
before a recharge is needed."

His finger flicked across the smartphone's screen. "There
are a whole bunch of other apps, like Mission Status, Threat
Level and SOS—that's my *own* program," Amir said proudly.

"So it worked!" Connor said. "Can you tell me what it's for
now?"

"Real emergencies," Amir replied, his expression serious.
"Even when you don't have a phone signal, the SOS app can
send a short burst of location data to a GPS satellite, and it's
bounced back here to headquarters. Works *anywhere* in the
world. Drains the battery like crazy, mind you. I'm still trying
to fix that. But you can explore all these apps when you're on
the plane. I've also added the latest Angry Birds game in case
you get bored."

"Not much chance of that!" replied Connor.

Amir laid the smartphone gently on the table, seeming

almost reluctant to let it go. Connor knew his friend was a bit of a tech-head and was dying to keep it for himself.

"That's the showpiece," Amir sighed, returning to the bag. "The other items I've prepped include a basic medical kit, a mini–halogen flashlight, prepaid credit cards and this set of clothes for high-threat situations."

Alongside the rest of the gear, he laid a baseball hat, a pair of sunglasses, a black T-shirt, a cream-colored dress shirt and a styled leather jacket.

"Jody promises me that they'll fit. Why not try them on for size?"

Connor slipped on the jacket. The cut was perfect, the quality equal to top-brand Italian leather, but the weight was odd.

"Feels a little ... heavy," he remarked.

"That's because it's bulletproof," explained Amir. "Both this and the shirt can stop a handgun at close range. The jacket's stab-proof too, as is this T-shirt."

Connor took a moment to inspect the clothes more closely. His fingers felt the thick cotton-like fabric of the collared shirt. "Are you sure this will stop a bullet?"

Amir nodded with the utmost conviction. "You can ask Jody, but I wouldn't recommend it."

"Why not?"

"When I did, she shot me."

"*What?*" exclaimed Connor, not sure he'd heard right.

Amir lifted his shirt to reveal a purple bruise across his chest. "She got me to wear one. It's constructed from a high-tech woven fabric that 'catches' the bullet and spreads the impact over the whole torso rather than in one specific area. So I can guarantee you—on my life—that the shirt works."

"I bet that hurt, though," said Connor, grimacing as Amir re-covered his bruised chest.

"I'd be lying if I said no. It felt like a battering ram. But at the time I was more worried about the contents of my pants! She scared me half to death. I'm *never* going to hand in homework late again."

Amir began to repack the bag for him.

"It's all right. I've already got my own backpack," said Connor.

"Not like this one you haven't," he replied. "This backpack could save your life too." He tapped the rear panel, then flexed it. "State-of-the-art liquid body armor. The jacket and shirt are only effective against handguns. This backpack will shield you from high-powered assault rifles and machine guns like the MP5."

"That's reassuring to know," said Connor, hoping he wouldn't be confronted by that sort of firepower.

"Colonel Black spares no expense on our safety equipment," explained Amir, showing Connor how the panel folded out to double its coverage. Then he resumed packing the bag.

Connor was astonished by the gear at his disposal. State-of-the-art phones, bulletproof clothing, anti-ambush backpacks. "I feel like James Bond," he said, picking up the snazzy pair of sunglasses with dark mirrored lens. "So what do these do?"

Connor was hoping for a "heads-up" display with augmented reality like the heroes used in the movies.

"Now these are *really* clever—one hundred percent anti-radiation, anti-glare devices," explained Amir, slipping them on and grinning. "They keep the sun out of your eyes!"

27

The Gulfstream jet touched down on the runway and taxied to the small private air terminal. As its engines wound down, the passenger door opened and the steps automatically unfolded. An immaculately presented flight attendant checked that the exit was clear before ushering the sole passenger from the plane.

"Thank you for flying with us," she said with a well-practiced smile of service, then added in farewell, "*Ma'as-salama.*"

"*Allah ysalmak,*" replied the man in his native Arabic, his amber eyes admiring the attractive woman one last time. Stepping onto the tarmac, he felt a wave of heat that was pleasant but by no means comparable to the arid warmth of his own country.

An airport official greeted him. "Sir, if you'd like to follow me."

They walked the short distance to the terminal building.

A pair of glass doors slid efficiently open and they were met by a blast of cold, air-conditioned air. Once the two were inside, the doors closed behind them, sealing out the noise of the whirring jet engines. The lobby was virtually deserted, with only a few employees milling about. A large flat-screen TV on the wall was running CNN in the background, the news coverage following the increased tension in the Arabian Peninsula over the recent oil blockade.

Crossing the thickly carpeted floor, the man was escorted over to Passport Control. A lone US Customs and Border Protection officer sat in his cubicle, his face fixed with a courteous but aloof expression.

"Passport," he said in a detached monotone.

The traveler handed over his documentation, and the officer swiped it into his computer. He inspected the monitor. "Welcome, Mr. Khalid Al . . ."

"Khalid Al-Naimi," the man said helpfully.

"And today you've come from . . . ?"

"Saudi Arabia," he replied, wondering why travelers were required to fill out such details on an I-94 form if passport officials never looked at them.

"What is the purpose of your visit? Business or pleasure?"

"Business," he replied. "Although, with any luck, it'll be pleasurable too."

The officer's dour expression failed to register the good-natured reply.

"And how long do you intend to stay?"

"No more than a month."

The officer swiveled a webcam to focus on the man's face. "Please look into the camera."

An image of a late-middle-aged Arab man with a silver-gray beard and amber eyes filled the screen. The officer took a photo, then gestured toward a black-and-green box fixed to the cubicle. "Now place your fingers on the scanner."

Putting down his briefcase, the man laid his right hand across the green plastic. Then his thumb.

The officer reexamined the details that appeared on his monitor. "What type of business are you in, Mr. Al-Naimi?"

"Oil."

The officer nodded, the answer seemingly of no interest to him despite his eyes flicking to the newscast. For a brief moment, he appeared reluctant to authorize the visitor's entry visa. But then he stamped the passport and returned the documents. With the formalities complete, he waved him through. "Welcome to the United States. Enjoy your stay."

The Arab man smiled. "I intend to."

He passed the inspection station and baggage claim without further security screening. His luggage had already been transferred, and his driver was waiting for him. Stepping outside into the bright sunshine, he was guided toward a blacked-out limousine by the chauffeur. The driver held open the rear passenger door, and the man slid into the plush leather seat. Once the door was closed, he was plunged into air-conditioned, shaded privacy.

With a casual yet careful look around the airport parking lot, the driver got behind the wheel and pulled away from the terminal.

"Pleasant flight, sir?" asked the driver as they joined the highway heading north to Washington, DC.

In the back, the Arab man was peeling off the first layer of skin from his right hand. The micro-thin latex parted to expose his real fingerprints.

"Yes, Hazim," replied Malik, now removing the colored contact lenses and returning his eyes from amber to their natural coal black. Later he would wash the silver dye from his beard too and trim it back. "And Bahir was right—security is relaxed at this private airport."

28

The black limousine passed the manned checkpoint and rolled along Pennsylvania Avenue. The grandiose, gray-granite Eisenhower Executive Office Building gave way to tall trees and an oasis of green that was Lafayette Square. Ahead, tourists wandered the wide leafy avenue, mostly ignoring the tiny encampment of peace protesters on the curb. Rather, their attention was on a stately building set back from the road by a run of iron railings. The modest palisade appeared to be the only barrier to the most famous address in America: the White House.

But Connor knew differently. As he peered through the limo's tinted window, his observant eye immediately spotted the snipers hidden on the roof. During his operational briefing, Colonel Black had informed him that these gunmen could hit a target accurately at more than a thousand yards. Connor was only a few hundred away, and with their shooting skill, he was the equivalent of a sitting duck.

Yet these weren't the only security measures in place. Although the White House appeared open and welcoming to the public, it was actually an impregnable fortress. All the windows were bullet-resistant. Guard stations controlled every entrance and exit. Vibration alarms beneath the lawn warned of fence jumpers, and infrared sensors aboveground detected any unwanted intruders. Then there were the teams of Secret Service agents patrolling the gardens. Often out of sight but always on the alert, these dedicated emergency-response units packed semi-automatic pistols, shotguns and even submachine guns.

With this level of protection, Connor wondered why the president needed him in the first place.

As the driver pulled up to the gated entrance of the White House, it was a surreal moment. Connor had seen the place countless times on TV, and it was almost as familiar as Big Ben or the London Eye. But he'd never imagined that one day he'd actually be visiting it, let alone working there. Barely twenty-four hours ago, he was in London saying good-bye to his mum and gran. They'd been told he was going on a summer exchange program in recognition for his out-standing grades. His mother had been delighted, the news seeming to give her a new lease on life. His gran had been more reserved. She had just whispered, "Be careful, Connor."

The gates parted, and the limo eased along the curving driveway toward the magnificent white-pillared entrance of the White House Residence. But shortly before it, the car bore right to arrive at the West Wing, the building that housed the official offices of the president of the United States. Pulling up beneath the roofed portico, the driver unlocked the doors and the Secret Service agent in the front passenger seat got out. With swift efficiency, he opened Connor's side.

"Welcome to the White House," he said. "The driver will see to your bags."

Connor stepped out, still a touch overwhelmed by his ceremonious welcome. He'd been flown business class, collected by stretch limousine and treated with the utmost courtesy. He felt more like a distinguished guest than a prospective bodyguard.

A single US Marine stood sentry outside the main doors. Still as a statue, he was dressed in full regalia, his boots polished like mirrors, his gloves spotlessly white. With regimented grace, he greeted their arrival and opened the doors to the lobby.

Connor followed the Secret Service agent inside. The white marble-floor entrance turned to plush carpet as they passed through a second set of double doors into the West Wing's official reception room. Furnished with red leather chairs and a pair of richly upholstered couches, the room was both elegant and intimate, like that of a top-class hotel. It boasted a collection of eighteenth-century oil paintings and an antique mahogany bookcase that took pride of place along the main wall.

"If you'd kindly wait here," instructed the agent. "I'll inform them of your arrival."

Connor was left in the room with another nameless agent, who stood silent but attentive next to a glass-topped reception desk. Several people passed through the lobby. The majority were too engrossed in their work to pay Connor much attention. But a couple raised eyebrows at the young teenager loitering in the reception area.

Connor also began to wonder what he was doing here. The initial thrill of his arrival in America had faded, and the underlying doubt about his abilities returned. Looking around the West Wing's luxurious reception room, he realized he was completely out of his depth. The truth was he was just a kid from the East End of London—albeit one with a kickboxing title to his name and twelve weeks of basic close-protection training. But surely that didn't qualify him for the responsibility of protecting the president's daughter. At some point, the powers-that-be were bound to discover he was a bodyguard in name only. That he was a *fraud*. And the consequences of his failure would be unthinkable. Not only would Colonel Black's Guardian organization be discredited, but he could put Alicia Mendez's life in real danger.

Just as he was considering bolting for the exit, a paneled wooden door opened and an elderly woman in a plaid suit and steel-rimmed glasses appeared.

"The president will see you now."

29

Connor stepped into the Oval Office. For a moment, he was convinced he'd walked onto a movie set, the scene instantly recognizable from so many movies. The ellipse-shaped room with its three floor-to-ceiling windows. The two ceremonial flags—the Stars and Stripes and the president's blue coat of arms—stationed like dutiful guards on either side. The polished oak-and-walnut floor covered by the iconic oval-shaped rug that proudly bore the presidential seal. And taking main stage, in front of the bow windows, was the famous ornately carved wooden desk at which the president of the United States sat.

Upon coming face-to-face with the man himself, Connor could only stare. His natural presence seemed to fill the room. Blessed with bronzed skin and well-defined cheekbones, President Mendez maintained a youthful yet worldly-wise look. His dark brown eyes were at once alert and deeply intense, giving Connor the impression that the president

rarely missed much. He wore a crisp blue suit with a bur-
gundy silk tie, and when the president stood, he was much
taller than he appeared on TV.

"It's a pleasure to meet you, Connor," said President
Mendez in a voice smooth as honey.

He extended his hand in welcome. Connor accepted it
and found his own enveloped by the heartfelt handshake.

"Thank you . . . Mr. P-President," he replied, stuttering. "It's
good to meet you too."

On the short walk through the West Wing's corridors, the
president's secretary had instructed him on the correct form
of address and encouraged him not to be afraid to speak up,
the president being a good-natured and gracious man. In
the small waiting area just outside the office, a Secret Service
agent had asked him to hand over his phone as a security
precaution before allowing Connor to enter.

"Please join us for coffee," said the president, gesturing toward three men standing between a pair of velvet upholstered
couches. "This is George Taylor, my White House chief of staff.
He's responsible for pretty much running the show here."

A man with a trimmed white beard and glasses stepped
forward. He greeted Connor with a smile. "It's good to have
you on the team."

"And this is General Martin Shaw, who originally recommended your Guardian organization."

Connor shook hands. "Colonel Black sends his regards."

"Why, thank you," replied the general in a thick Texan accent. Big as a bear and impeccably turned out in his olive-green uniform, he displayed the same military bearing as his English counterpart. "It's just a shame the colonel couldn't join us."

The president introduced the remaining member of the group, a thin man with gray-flecked hair and crow's-feet spreading out from his steel-blue eyes. "And, finally, the director of the Secret Service, Dirk Moran."

"Pleased to meet you," said Connor, offering his hand. "I've been told I'm reporting to you."

"That's right," the director replied. His handshake was brief and cool, and Connor got the feeling he was being appraised right from the start.

They all sat as the chief of staff poured the coffee. Although he didn't actually like coffee, Connor accepted a cup out of politeness.

"Is this your first time in the States?" asked President Mendez, dropping a lump of sugar into his drink.

Connor nodded. "But I like what I've seen so far."

"And what would that be?" asked Dirk.

"Well, the White House. It's certainly well protected," replied Connor and, wanting to impress, added, "Snipers, bullet-resistant glass, hidden cameras, infrared sensors . . ."

The general raised a wry eyebrow in Dirk's direction. "The boy's done his research."

"In fact, I was surprised I wasn't searched on arrival," finished Connor.

The president looked to his director for an explanation of this apparent lapse in security.

"That's because you were scanned discreetly as you passed through the lobby," explained Dirk. "You don't know *all* our security measures, young man. No one ever does."

"Sometimes not even the president himself!" President Mendez said, laughing as he put down his coffee cup. "President Eisenhower once said, 'America is best described by one word: *freedom*.' And that is true. But Thomas Jefferson, our third president and Founding Father, also observed that 'the price of freedom is eternal vigilance.' Unfortunately, in this day and age, vigilance isn't only a byword, it's a way of life. Especially for the president and the first family. We need constant, round-the-clock protection from the Secret Service."

He sighed, the weight of office momentarily seeming a burden rather than an honor.

"This can be hard to live with, day in, day out. Which is why my daughter has taken exception to such imposing protection. And why the Guardian's services have been requested."

No longer able to contain the burning question that had been on his mind ever since his selection, Connor put down his undrunk cup of coffee and asked, "Why did you choose *me*?"

President Mendez clasped his hands almost as if in prayer. "I would have thought that was obvious. Your father saved my life."

Connor's jaw dropped. *"When? How?"*

The president sat back, surprised at his reaction. "Has no one ever told you that?"

"No," admitted Connor. "I was just told my dad was killed in an ambush in Iraq and that he died a hero."

"That's correct. He gave his life to rescue *me.*"

The president then recounted his trip to Iraq six years previously as US ambassador. How the British and American forces were working together to secure peace and that an SAS detachment had been assigned to help protect high-profile visiting diplomats. He spoke with passion about his miraculous escape from the attack on their convoy and how Connor's father had risked it all to ensure his safety.

Connor listened, rapt. This was the first time he'd heard the details of his father's heroic act. But it explained the Soldier's Medal—the one embossed with the American eagle—that was among the possessions his mother kept in a "memory box." She'd always been too distraught to talk about his father's death, and as he'd grown older, he'd stopped asking about it. But at last, he knew the whole story.

As the president came to the end, he slid a small scratched key fob across the coffee table to Connor.

"I kept this to remind myself of the true meaning of sacrifice," he explained. "To ensure that I lived a life of sacrifice for my country as their president. Your father held this in his hand as he died. And now I return it to you."

Connor stared down at his father's talisman. From beneath the plastic, a picture of a familiar eight-year-old boy smiled up at him.

"In my eyes, Justin Reeves was a very courageous, loyal and noble soldier," said President Mendez earnestly. "And you have his blood running through your veins. Which is why I'd trust my daughter's life only to a Reeves guardian."

Connor was speechless, choked with emotion and grief at the account of his father's selfless bravery.

Seeing the effect his words had, the president said, "I'll understand perfectly if you feel you can't accept this role, Connor." His expression was kindly and sincere, yet at the same time hopeful. "But I would sleep more soundly in my bed knowing Alicia is truly safe—protected not only by the Secret Service, but by you."

Connor stared at the key fob. His *dad's* key fob. Losing a father was a pain no one should have to bear. But in his father's case, could it possibly be deemed "worth it"? He'd saved the life of a man who went on to become the president of the United States. A leader who was being hailed as a new dawn for America, according to what Connor had read about him. A visionary who could steer the country to peace and prosperity. And all this was possible *only* because of his father. Connor felt an immense sense of pride in him.

Gripping the key fob, Connor said, "I can assure you, Mr. President, I'll do my best to protect your daughter."

"That's all I ask of anyone," replied President Mendez, smiling warmly.

"Now, Connor, remember your assignment is to be kept confidential," the White House chief of staff said. "Aside from those of us in this room, a few key Secret Service agents and the first lady, no one will know your true purpose."

"And Alicia, of course?" added Connor.

Dirk intervened, "No, you'll be introduced to her later as a special guest of the president on an exchange program. The White House has done such exchanges before, so it won't raise suspicion."

"So Alicia won't know I'm guarding her?" Connor asked.

"Ideally not," replied the president. "With any luck, she'll think she's looking after *you*."

30

"Over ten thousand death threats a year are made against the president and his family," Dirk Moran said as he led Connor down another windowless and indistinguishable corridor.

After his meeting with President Mendez, Connor had been driven with the director to an unmarked building in downtown DC. Although it looked like any other office on the street, it actually housed the headquarters of the Secret Service. Having been issued a security pass, Connor was then escorted by the director deep into the labyrinthine complex.

"That's *thirty* potential attacks every day," Dirk emphasized in a grave tone. "Each and every one has to be investigated." They passed a busy office to their left. "In there, the members of our Intelligence Division are tasked with differentiating between those who make threats and those capable of carrying out such threats. Then the agency's job is to prevent any viable threat from becoming a full-blown attack."

They came to an unmarked door, and the director stopped.

"Before we go any farther, Connor," he said, his expression hardening, "I need you to understand something."

Reaching into his jacket pocket, Dirk pulled out a slim black leather wallet.

"Our mandate is to *Protect the man. Protect the symbol. Protect the office.* And the Secret Service's Presidential Protective Division is the last line of defense," he explained.

With a flick, he snapped the wallet open in front of Connor's face. Inside was a golden badge with an eagle on the top. At its center was the American Stars and Stripes, the miniature flag surrounded by a five-pointed star. Above and below the star were emblazoned the words *United States Secret Service.*

"This badge represents years of training, dedication and experience in the service of the president. As the director of the Secret Service, I do *not* gamble with the lives of the first family." His voice was taut with barely constrained fury. "And no young upstart—whose only qualifications are a few weeks' training and a bodyguard for a father—will jeopardize our mission!"

Connor was taken aback by the unexpected tirade. "If you don't want me here, why did you invite me in the first place?"

"I didn't," replied Dirk through clenched teeth as he pocketed his badge. "I consider you a liability. But I have to obey the president's wishes. Be warned, though: if you make a *single* mistake that compromises the safety of the first daughter, you'll be flying home quicker than you can say 'Secret Service.' Do I make myself clear?"

Although intimidated by the man's hostility, Connor was determined to prove the director's assumptions wrong. "Perfectly clear."

"Good. Point made," said Dirk, regaining his professional composure and offering a thin smile. "Now, if you're to work alongside us, you need to know *how* we work."

Sliding a key card through an electronic slot, he pushed open the door to reveal a large room humming with state-of-the-art equipment. There were wall-to-wall monitors, two massive overhead screens, a digital banner displaying a constant flow of live data, and several black cubicles, each with their own terminal and communications port. A small team of agents worked quietly and efficiently, processing the incoming information.

"The Joint Operations Center," declared Dirk with some pride. "This is where we track the movements of the president and the first family. It contains information so sensitive that only a select few are allowed access. So feel privileged."

Following the director inside, Connor passed a row of monitors displaying multiple views of a familiar white building and large garden. Two men were stationed at desks, analyzing the images.

"The White House is under constant surveillance," explained Dirk. "Every entrance, every approach and every exit is covered. Even the air around the White House is monitored twenty-four hours a day."

They headed over to the first cubicle. The agent manning the desk nodded respectfully at the director. "Sir."

"Agent Greenaway here is responsible for tracking the first lady."

The agent gestured toward a street map displayed on his screen. A green dot traced a route along one of the roads. "The first lady often goes on diplomatic and humanitarian trips abroad," Greenaway explained. "Her car has just left the hotel and is heading southeast on the Champs-Élysées in Paris."

A message flashed up on the monitor: NIGHTOWL ARRIVING AT BLUE 1. FIVE MINUTES.

Connor gave the agent a questioning look. "Is 'Nightowl' her call sign?"

The agent nodded. "To maintain secrecy with radio communications, each member of the first family is assigned a code name."

"What are the others?" asked Connor.

"Code names are kept confidential," said Dirk pointedly. "If and when the press gets wind of them, they're changed effective immediately."

"But surely I need to know them in case I have to report any problems."

Dirk gave a begrudging nod. "I suppose so. Currently President Mendez is known as Ninja, for his love of old martial arts movies. The first lady is Nightowl, because she stays up late. And Alicia's call sign is Nomad."

"*Nomad?*" repeated Connor.

"Well, she's always wandering off!" Agent Greenaway said, laughing.

The director cut short the agent's amusement with a sharp disciplinary look.

"We've also given you a call sign, Connor," Dirk revealed.

"Really?" said Connor, looking hopeful.

"Yes, to reflect your role in our operation."

"What is it?"

"Bandit," he replied with a smirk.

Connor was coming to realize that, although Dirk wouldn't actively prevent him from doing his job, he certainly wouldn't be helping him either. He'd have to tread very carefully with the director if he was going to succeed in this operation.

Dirk directed him over to a central bank of monitors. "In the event of a crisis, the standard operating procedure is to ensure that every protectee is moved quickly and safely to a secure site—a safe house. These will depend upon your location at the time of the crisis." He pointed to one of the screens. "This is a feed from the National Terrorism Advisory System. It's a two-tier alert listing credible threats. These are classified as either *Elevated* or *Imminent* and are accompanied by a summary of the threat and the actions recommended to be taken. Along with the information from the Intelligence Division, this dictates our protection protocol for the first family."

Connor studied the scrolling list of alerts. "There seem to be a lot of them."

"We have al-Qaeda to thank for that," replied the director bitterly. "Although America has dealt with terrorism throughout its history, 9/11 changed everything. We're now up against a modern strain of the threat, one that has no boundaries. Attacks can be violent, indiscriminate and crippling. It's very hard to defend against an enemy who lives by the code *The Gates of Paradise are under the shadows of the swords.*"

His finger tapped the screen pensively as threat after threat scrolled by.

"Terrorists are like the mythical beast Hydra—you cut one head off and two grow in its place. The threat constantly looms. Someone, somewhere, always wants to kill the president or his family."

31

Hazim checked his watch as two black Cadillac limousines rolled up to the school gates: 2:48.

The security guard in the kiosk waved them through. With rehearsed precision, they followed the driveway and stopped outside the main building just as the school bell sounded: 2:50.

A broad-shouldered man in a suit and dark glasses stepped out of the front passenger seat. Tucked behind his left ear was the telltale curly wire of a two-way radio. With a brief yet thorough scan of his surroundings, he headed for the glass doors of the main entrance. Meanwhile, three more men exited the rear vehicle and took up their stations around the front limo—two at the right-hand corners and one on the road facing out, so that all the observation arcs were covered.

The Not-So Secret Service! thought Hazim drily, the agents standing out like sore thumbs among the other arriving parents. A slight bulge on each man's right hip hinted at the concealed SIG Sauer P229 pistol that they all carried as standard issue. And on the lapel of their suits gleamed the small but distinctive hexagonal badge with its five-pointed star of the Secret Service.

Hazim took note of all these details from behind his sunglasses while he searched for weaknesses in the functioning of the protection team. Malik had told him that arriving or leaving a location was the most vulnerable point in any security operation—even more so for the daily school run. The timing of arrival and departure was always known. The drop-off and pickup points were always the same. And whatever route the limos took to and from the White House, they had to end or start at the Montarose School. It made this the most likely snatch point.

The first of the students began spilling out of the entrance, a few walking home, most being picked up in cars. The agents kept a wary eye out for strangers. But this didn't concern Hazim as he continued his covert surveillance.

At 2:53, a dark-haired girl—the one they'd *all* been waiting for—walked out of the glass doors with a group of friends. Three girls. They chatted and giggled on the steps for a minute or so. Then, waving good-bye, Alicia Mendez made her way to the front limo.

Two paces behind on her right followed the first Secret Service agent. As soon as she was safely inside the limo and the door closed, the agent jumped into the front passenger seat and the driver pulled away. The escort vehicle quickly moved forward, collected the other agents and sped after them: 2:55.

The whole embarkation process from door to car had taken less than sixty seconds. Hazim realized the window of opportunity was very small. Possibly too small. But that was for his uncle Malik to decide.

Hazim's eyes followed the lead limo as it pulled out of the school drive and turned left onto Wisconsin Avenue. The two vehicles merged with the Washington traffic: 2:56.

Hazim didn't make any attempt to pursue them. He simply thumbed a coded text on his phone:

Eagle Chick flying south.

A few moments later his phone pinged in reply, a message flashing on the screen.

Gamekeeper has the eyeball on Eagle Chick.

32

Alicia sat on the leather chair, kicking her heels against the soft beige carpet of the president's outer office. She absently surfed the Internet on her smartphone, then sent several text messages to her school friends. Glancing up at the clock on the wall, she sighed with boredom.

From behind her neatly arranged desk, Mrs. Holland, the president's secretary, offered an apologetic smile. "I'm sure your father won't be much longer, Alicia."

"You tell me that every time," Alicia replied, but not unkindly. Mrs. Holland, although fiercely loyal to the president and protective of his schedule, had become almost a surrogate grandmother to her within the confines of the White House.

"And I'm never wrong, am I?" said Mrs. Holland, peering over her steel-rimmed glasses as the door to the Oval Office opened and a tall woman with long dark-blond hair stepped out. She was dressed in a sleek blue business suit and carried a wafer-thin touch-screen computer. Alicia recognized her as Karen Wright, the newly appointed director of National Intelligence and her father's principal adviser on all matters related to the security of the United States.

"Thank you for the update, Karen," said President Mendez, appearing in the doorway. "Keep me informed of any developments."

"Of course, Mr. President. You'll be the first to know," replied Karen. Turning to leave, she smiled warmly at Alicia. "Hello, Alicia."

"Hi, Karen," she replied as the director disappeared down the corridor.

President Mendez now faced his daughter. "Sorry to keep you waiting, honey."

"Don't worry, I'm used to it," Alicia replied, picking up her schoolbag and following her father inside.

Feeling a twinge of parental guilt, President Mendez put an arm around his daughter and kissed the top of her head. "But *this* is the meeting I look forward to the most every day," he insisted.

Alicia's lips tightened as she bit back the urge to say, *Is that all I am to you . . . a meeting?*

They sat down together on the sofa. Alicia both enjoyed and hated these moments with her father in equal measure. She understood he was extremely busy as president and appreciated that he *always* made time for her in his hectic schedule. Yet their "meetings" were all too short and often felt like a duty rather than a relaxed personal moment between father and daughter.

"How was school?" President Mendez asked. "Has your protection team backed off?"

"I suppose so," she replied with a shrug. "They still hang around at breaks, though."

"Well, that's their job," he replied, his tone firm yet sympathetic. "Did you have dance class today?"

Alicia nodded. "Yeah, we're learning how to salsa."

President Mendez smiled warmly as a fond memory washed over him. "Your mother's a great salsa dancer. It's a shame she's not here to teach you a few moves."

Alicia glanced up at him hopefully. "When's she getting back?"

"Still at the end of the month, I'm afraid."

Groaning, Alicia slumped back against the cushions of the sofa. "She's been gone *forever*."

"Hey, believe me, I'm missing her too," said President Mendez, pulling his daughter into a hug. "But I have a surprise to keep you company in the meantime."

Alicia visibly perked up at this. She'd been begging her parents for a puppy for weeks, and looked up at her father expectantly.

"We have a special young guest coming to stay for the summer, maybe longer," he announced.

The hopeful look on Alicia's face faded as fast as it had appeared. This wasn't about a puppy. Far from it.

"Not *again*!" she exclaimed, recalling the last "special guest" who had visited on an exchange the previous year—the vain and morose daughter of some visiting French dignitary. Despite Alicia's numerous attempts to make friends, the girl had remained aloof and constantly complained about everything from food to fashion to the weather. It had been even more painful to have her in the same class and hanging around with her friends. When the girl had finally returned home, Alicia couldn't have been happier.

President Mendez gave his daughter a stern look. "I'm sure I needn't remind you, Alicia, of your obligation as the president's daughter to welcome guests to our country."

"Yeah, but not babysit them!" she retorted, crossing her arms.

"Well, if you're not interested, I can always cancel the visit," said the president nonchalantly. "I just thought having a guy your age around the White House would make a nice change."

Alicia struggled not to let her jaw drop open in shock. A boy? Her age? That was most unusual. Typically, her father was overprotective when it came to the subject of boys.

"No . . . it's okay," she backtracked, her interest now piqued. "So, who is he?"

"The son of an old and trusted friend I knew from my time in Iraq."

"He's an Iraqi?"

"No, he's English. His father was a soldier."

Trying hard not to appear too excited, Alicia began to inspect one of her fingernails for imaginary dirt. "When do I get to meet him?"

"As soon as you're ready. He's waiting for you in the Diplomatic Reception Room."

"What?" exclaimed Alicia, jumping up from the sofa and looking at her school clothes in horror. "I can't see him like *this!*"

President Mendez tried to suppress a smile as he watched his daughter dash out of the Oval Office toward the main residence to get changed. Diplomacy was one thing he excelled at, especially when it came to convincing people that certain decisions were their own.

33

Connor waited nervously in the large oval reception room on the ground floor of the White House. He was alone, apart from a discreet Secret Service agent, who stood stock-still and silent by a set of double doors as though he were part of the furniture. The soft gold-and-blue decor of the stately room did little to alleviate Connor's worries. Despite the distraction of the stunning panorama of American landscapes that circled the entire room, Connor couldn't help but feel apprehensive about his first encounter with the president's daughter.

How should I act? Formal or casual? Or should I just be myself? What am I going to say? And what if Alicia takes an instant dislike to me? How am I going to do my job then . . .

As all these concerns whirled through his mind, the double doors opened and President Mendez stepped through, followed by his daughter and two Secret Service agents.

"Connor, welcome to the White House," greeted the

president, warmly shaking his hand. "I'm so glad we could arrange your stay. Please allow me to introduce my daughter, Alicia."

For a moment, Connor was speechless. Alicia was even more attractive than the photos had suggested. Her striking sunflower-yellow dress made her bronze complexion almost seem to glow, and he found himself mesmerized by her deep brown eyes . . .

Connor pulled himself together. These weren't the thoughts of a professional bodyguard. He wasn't here to admire his Principal. He was here to protect her.

"Hi . . . I'm Connor," he finally managed to blurt out, and for some reason, he bowed.

"Pleased to meet you too," Alicia replied with an amused smile. "But there's no need to bow."

"Well . . . . you are the president's daughter."

"True, but I'm not royalty!"

Connor's cheeks flushed a little with embarrassment at his mistake in etiquette.

President Mendez glanced from one to the other and waited for either to say more. When neither did, he prompted, "Well, now that you've met, I suggest, Alicia, you give Connor a tour of our home."

Alicia nodded dutifully.

President Mendez turned to Connor and shook his hand. "Sorry I can't join you. I have to get back to running the country! But I do hope all goes well during your stay with us," he said, shooting Connor a knowing wink.

"Thank you, Mr. President," Connor replied as the great man took his leave, the two agents remaining behind.

Once Alicia's father was gone, there was a moment of awkward silence. Connor exchanged a strained smile with Alicia as they each tried to think of something to say.

Then Alicia began. "So . . . this is the Diplomatic Reception Room."

Her hand swept around the decorated walls.

"Um . . . Jacqueline Kennedy had this pictorial wallpaper put up in the sixties. That's Niagara Falls over there . . . New York Bay . . . Boston Harbor. And this old fireplace is where President Franklin Roosevelt broadcast his famous fireside chats."

Connor nodded politely. Although he'd never heard of Roosevelt's broadcasts, he was more than happy for Alicia to take him on a guided tour, since it gave him the opportunity to get to know her. As a bodyguard, it was important to quickly assess a Principal's character and manner so that one could work efficiently and agreeably with them.

"In the past, this room housed a furnace and boiler," she explained, "and before that, it was used by servants for polishing the silver."

Maintaining the formality of the occasion, Alicia guided him next door to the China Room and showed him its priceless displays of ivory-and-burnished-gold china. Next, they moved on to the Vermeil Room with its extensive collection of silver-gilt tableware; the wooden-paneled Library with its unusual lighthouse clock; and, to Connor's great surprise, a bowling alley in the basement. Then they climbed the Grand Staircase up to the State Floor. The first point of call was the East Room—a magnificent ceremonial hall with long gilded drapes, a marble fireplace and antique glass chandeliers hanging above a Steinway grand piano. As they traipsed through the furniture displays in the Green, Blue and Red Rooms, Connor was struggling to maintain his interest. Impressive as the White House was, there was only so much antiquity and artwork he could take.

Alicia noticed his eyes glazing over and stopped talking.

"Sorry," said Connor, attempting to stifle a yawn. "Must be jet lag."

But, rather than take offense, Alicia grinned at him. "Shall we skip the boring parts?"

Connor nodded eagerly. "If you don't mind."

"Not at all," she said, visibly relaxing in his presence. "To be honest, I hate doing these official tours. I just thought that was what you expected as an official guest."

"No, I'd prefer to do what *you* want," Connor replied.

"Cool," said Alicia, smiling. "Then I hope you don't scare easily!"

34

"You mean, he could be watching us *right now*?" said Connor, unnerved by Alicia's story. The two of them had headed for the infamous Lincoln Bedroom on the second floor. He scanned the room and looked out through the window at the slowly setting sun.

Alicia nodded, her face drawn into a mask of fright. "Don't you feel his *presence*?" Her voice was almost a whisper, her dark eyes wide as she pointed a trembling finger toward the door. "I think . . . that's him . . ."

Connor could see a faint shadow moving along the narrow gap at the foot of the wooden door. Silently, he crept across the plush emerald-green carpet. His fingers clasped the brass handle; it was cool to the touch. The movement outside ceased. With a quick twist, Connor yanked the door open, and a startled Secret Service agent leaped away in shock.

"That's not Abraham Lincoln's ghost!" Connor exclaimed with a grin.

Alicia laughed as the agent recovered his wits. "No, but it could have been. Over the years, numerous sightings have been recorded. President Reagan's first daughter said she saw Lincoln standing at that window peering out across the lawn. Harry Truman, the thirty-third president, once wrote in a letter that he heard footsteps up and down the hallway at night, as well as knocking on his door, when no one was there. Winston Churchill even refused to sleep in this room after coming face-to-face with Lincoln's ghost. The White House is *definitely* haunted."

"Aren't you scared?" asked Connor.

"A little," admitted Alicia. "But he's a friendly ghost . . . I think."

Connor examined a holograph copy of the Gettysburg Address, President Lincoln's best-known speech, displayed on a desk by the window. "It must be amazing to live in the White House," he remarked.

Alicia smiled proudly. "Yes, and the Mendez family are now part of its history."

Then she lowered her voice to a conspiratorial whisper so that the Secret Service agent outside in the hallway wouldn't overhear. "But to be honest, Connor, sometimes I hate it. It's a museum, not a home. I'm almost too scared to touch something in case I break it! And thousands of people come through the house on tours every month. It's not like I can leave my things anywhere I want."

She glanced toward the agent.

"And there's no privacy either. A Secret Service agent is stationed in almost every room. Sometimes I think *they're* the ghosts—haunting my every step."

Connor smiled sympathetically. "It must be hard," he said. Although he realized that if anyone was a ghost, *he* was—as her secret bodyguard.

"You don't know the half of it. It's like living in a cross between a reform school and a convent." She laughed weakly at her comparison. "Just going to meet my friends to hang out is a mission in itself. Literally *anything* I want to do outside the White House requires advanced planning by the Secret Service."

Alicia sighed, then shrugged in a what-can-you-do-about-it way.

"Sorry, you don't want to be hearing all this," she said, perching herself on the end of the Lincoln bed.

"No, it's fine," replied Connor.

"It's just that I don't often have many people my own age around here and . . . you seem pretty easy to get along with. I do realize how fortunate I am. I mean, the White House has its own movie theater, bowling alley and swimming pool. And I get to meet some truly amazing people—kings and queens, heads of state, famous musicians and movie stars. I have to pinch myself at times. I even met the Dalai Lama once. He told me, 'Happiness is not something ready-made.

It comes from your own actions.'" Alicia quickly cheered at the thought. "And there are a *few* rooms in the White House where I can be left alone. Come on, I'll show you my favorite."

She led Connor out of the Lincoln Bedroom and up the stairs to the third floor, the agent discreetly following behind. This level, as Connor already knew, was where the first family relaxed and also where the guest bedrooms were housed, a maid having shown him to his room earlier.

As they turned left up a ramped hallway, the agent stopped shadowing them. The two of them entered the solarium, a private chill-out space with comfy sofas and glass walls that offered unbroken views of the Washington skyline.

"Welcome to the fishbowl!" announced Alicia. "This is about as free as it gets."

Opening a patio door, she stepped out onto the rooftop terrace. She took a deep breath and opened her arms.

"FREEDOM!" she cried.

But Connor only saw the high stone balustrade that shielded the terrace and solarium from general view. Glancing up at the apex of the roof, he caught a brief glimpse of a black-uniformed sniper. Then he peered between the thick white pillars of the balustrade at the expanse of the South Lawn. From his vantage point, he could spy the Secret Service agents patrolling the grounds and the boundary fence where swarms of tourists gathered in the hope of spotting the first family.

Connor began to understand Alicia's plight. The White House was as much a prison as a home. No wonder she was desperate to escape the perpetual shadow of the Secret Service. She was like a bird trapped in a gilded cage.

35

Connor had never arrived at school in such style. Cushioned by soft leather seats and comforted in air-conditioned luxury, he and Alicia were driven through the downtown Washington traffic right up to the steps of Montarose School's main building. After a brief surveillance sweep by Secret Service, the limo doors unlocked and he and Alicia were ushered from the car like movie stars.

"We'll collect you at 1500 hours," said the broad-shouldered agent with a courteous smile.

"As always, Kyle," Alicia replied, waving good-bye.

Kyle, as Connor had discovered, was the primary bodyguard in the first daughter's protection team. He was also one of the few select agents to be aware of Connor's role—and, surprisingly, the most receptive to it. Upon being introduced, Kyle had taken the time to explain the team's key security procedures and action-on drills. He'd even covered details such as the small hexagonal lapel badges all Secret

Service agents wore. These were a security measure; their color routinely changed to reduce the likelihood of infiltration by an outsider.

As Connor stepped from the limo, Kyle gave him a subtle nod as if to say, *Over to you now.*

Connor knew he wasn't being left entirely alone in his close-protection duties. The grounds of the private school were security patrolled and cordoned off with high fences. Also the Secret Service agents would be stationed just a short distance away throughout the day. But, that said, Alicia's immediate safety was now in his hands.

Connor followed Alicia up the steps into the main foyer. The corridors were packed with students.

"Alicia!" cried a voice, and three girls came running over just as Connor finished signing in at reception.

They all embraced and kissed one another's cheeks.

A black girl with a bundle of dark hair and a diamond-white smile glanced over Alicia's shoulder. "Is that the English boy you were talking about last night?"

Alicia nodded.

"Cute," the girl whispered to her friends, and they giggled.

Connor offered an embarrassed smile. "Hi there."

"Ooh," sighed a girl with long blond hair tied up in a pony-tail. "Say something else."

Connor frowned in puzzlement. "Like what?"

"Anything."

Connor shrugged. "It's nice to meet you. What's your name?"

The girl clapped her hands in delight. "I just *love* that English accent," she cooed. "I'm Paige. You can talk to me like that all day."

"And I'm Grace," said the black girl, dazzling him with her smile.

Alicia urged her other friend forward. "This is Kalila," she said, introducing a girl with olive skin and almond eyes, who wore a light purple hijab.

"Hello," she said, her voice soft as a breeze.

"Hi," replied Connor. "Are you all in Alicia's class?"

The girls nodded.

"Connor's joining our class for the rest of the semester," explained Alicia.

"Cool!" said Grace. "You can sit next to *me*."

Alicia's eyes flashed her friend a good-natured warning. "Connor can sit where he wants."

"But there's a spare seat right beside me," replied Grace innocently.

Connor looked to Alicia. "Um, where will you be sitting?"

"I'd be right in front of you."

"Well, that sounds fine," he replied casually. In fact, the positioning was perfect. From the perspective of a bodyguard, he could protect her back if necessary, observe any threat approaching from the front and easily grab her to provide body cover or escape in the event of an emergency.

Alicia's schoolbag buzzed, and she pulled out her cell phone to read the text message.

"Hey, that's a cool phone case!" said Paige.

Alicia grinned, pleased that one of her friends had noticed. "It's a present from Connor."

"Lucky you—that's a limited-edition Armani!" Grace exclaimed, admiring the red butterfly logo.

The girls crowded around to have a better look.

"Just a thank-you gift," explained Connor, worried they'd read too much into it. But the girls were more interested in comparing phone cases and lucky charms.

The school bell rang for class.

"Come on," said Alicia, grabbing her bag and looking at Connor. "First period is history. If you can survive this, you can survive anything!"

36

History wasn't one of Connor's favorite subjects, but the class was made even more challenging by the double life he was leading. Protecting the president's daughter meant he had to be on constant alert—Code Yellow. But that was hard to maintain when a teacher was asking questions and there was classwork to be done. It was only his first day, and Connor already felt like he was performing a constant juggling act with his attention.

The open window. The teacher. The other students. Alicia. The unanswered workbook on his desk. The person passing in the corridor . . .

As the bell sounded for lunch, after the first three periods of history, Mandarin Chinese and math, Connor was glad to be able to concentrate on just one role—that of being a guardian.

Alicia and her friends collected their bags and headed for

the cafeteria with Connor in tow. As they wandered down the corridor, Connor kept a careful eye out for potential threats. Although it was tempting to relax—since they were within the relatively safe confines of a private school—Colonel Black had reinforced in him during training that "assumption is the mother of all screwups." A bodyguard could *never* assume that an area was totally safe or an individual was not a threat. Vigilance was required at all times. This meant that although the Secret Service would have vetted anyone in direct contact with Alicia, there was always a chance one shark could slip through the net. This could be a teacher; an office clerk; one of the kitchen staff, custodians or groundskeepers; a delivery driver; or even a fellow student. *Everyone* was a suspect.

But the threat need not be an assassination. As Alicia's bodyguard, Connor was to protect her from all forms of harm—from everyday bullying to a simple accident. So although he didn't expect there'd be any potential assassins among the students, if Montarose School was anything like his own in East London, there'd certainly be a bonehead or two.

As if on cue, two boys strolled up to their group as they waited in line for food. One was well built, with dark wavy hair, a square jaw and a confident swagger. He looked like a young Clark Kent who'd forgotten to put on his glasses and was still Superman. His friend was bigger—a bulldozer of a boy with a short crew cut and what looked to be size-ten Converse sneakers.

"Hey, Alicia!" drawled Superman. "What's up?"

"Hi, Ethan," she replied, smiling coyly as her friends gathered to one side to give them space. Then, "Ethan, this is Connor from England."

The boy gave a brief nod in Connor's direction. "Right!"

Then he turned his attention back to Alicia before Connor had a chance to reply. "So, what are you doing this weekend?" he asked.

Alicia glanced sideways at her giggling classmates. "My father's asked me to take Connor to the National Mall on Saturday. Want to join us?"

"Nah, it's just a bunch of old museums and monuments," snorted Ethan. "Anyway, I've got baseball practice."

"Ethan's the top hitter on the school team," Grace whispered to Connor, handing him a lunch tray. "He's also the star quarterback."

Connor nodded. Judging by the boy's attitude, he certainly thought himself a star.

"Are you going to the school dance?" Ethan asked casually.

"Maybe," replied Alicia, twirling a lock of dark hair around her finger. "Depends who's asking."

"I am."

Alicia pursed her lips. "I'll think about it."

"*Think about it?*" exclaimed Ethan, his stunned expression suggesting he never expected "no" from a girl—even the president's daughter. "It's only two weeks away."

"Yeah, but I need the Secret Service to check you out first. Got to confirm you're no 'threat,'" she said, raising her eyebrows teasingly.

"But I'm a senator's son!" he replied, clearly not getting Alicia's joke. He walked off in a huff, muttering, "Well, don't take too long to decide."

The girls regrouped around Alicia.

"I don't believe you!" said Paige, her blue eyes wide. "Ethan asked you to the school dance and you didn't say *yes*."

"He's got to work a bit harder than that," replied Alicia. "The guy needs some style first. He needs to impress me. I mean, he asked me in the lunch line, for goodness' sake!"

As the girls stood gossiping, Connor became aware of someone staring intently at Alicia through the glass pane of a door marked No Admittance. He couldn't make out the man's features clearly, since the glass was obscured. But the man's eyes were magnified by it, and his attention was definitely fixed on Alicia.

Connor's awareness shot up one level to Code Orange. As he evaluated the potential threat, the man noticed Connor looking in his direction, and suddenly disappeared.

"What's behind that door?" Connor asked Kalila.

"Just the kitchens," she replied, helping herself to a Caesar salad from the food bar.

"We'll sit over there, Connor," Alicia called, pointing to a table by the window.

"Right behind you," Connor replied, quickly selecting a sandwich and a drink. He hurried over to ensure he got a seat beside Alicia. He allowed his alert level to drop to Code Yellow again. But for her safety he wanted the best position to view the cafeteria and the No Admittance door—just in case the watcher made a second appearance.

37

During his afternoon classes, English and earth science, Connor pondered the face at the glass. If not for his body-guard training, he doubted he'd have noticed the man in the first place. There was no real reason to suspect anything more than a curious member of the kitchen staff. The face never reappeared and could simply have been a cook check-ing the length of the lunch line, or a new kitchen hand who'd had his first sighting of the president's daughter. But something about the intensity of the man's stare unsettled Connor. Perhaps it was the way the man's eyes had been magnified by the rippled glass, or the fact that he'd directed his gaze at Alicia alone and nobody else.

The school bell rang, interrupting his thoughts.

"Remember, I want your assignments on my desk by Fri-day," said Mr. Hulme, their earth science teacher, over the scrape of chairs and thumping of bags.

Connor wished he'd been paying more attention. He hurriedly scribbled down the assignment from the whiteboard as the students piled out of the classroom, eager to go home and enjoy what was left of the day's sunshine. Alicia waited for Connor, and they headed for the main foyer with her friends. At the end of the corridor, he held the door open for them.

"Thank you," said Alicia, surprised by his courteous gesture.

"Aww, English boys are so polite," said Paige, skipping through after her with Grace and Kalila.

Before Connor could follow, Ethan barged past. "Good work, doorman."

His friend, whose name Connor had discovered was Jimbo, also muscled his way through with no more than a grunt of acknowledgment. Connor held himself in check at their rudeness. He didn't want to get on the wrong side of *any* of Alicia's friends—even the most obnoxious. At the same time, he wasn't going to be pushed around.

"Next time leave a tip!" he cried, keeping his voice light and humorous.

Neither Ethan nor Jimbo bothered to reply.

Letting the door swing shut behind him, Connor instinctively checked over his shoulder. He noticed a man with black hair, glasses and a dark complexion standing at the far end of the corridor. He was staring intently in Alicia's direction. *Could this be the face behind the glass?* But the man wasn't dressed in kitchen-work clothes. He wore light-colored chinos, a shirt and a striped blue tie.

"Who's that?" asked Connor.

Alicia glanced back down the corridor. "Oh, that's Mr. Hayek, the new IT teacher. He must be on hall duty."

Connor let his guard down. He realized he was being *too* paranoid. If he continued to suspect everyone and anyone who merely looked at the president's daughter, he'd be a nervous wreck by the end of the week. He made a mental note to study the photos of the teachers and school staff that Ling had compiled in his operations folder. That way he need only be suspicious of strangers and any staff doing something out of the ordinary.

They congregated in the foyer to say good-bye.

"So who's up for the National Mall this weekend?" asked Alicia.

Grace smiled. "Sorry, seeing my grandparents."

"Catch you later for shopping maybe," said Paige.

"You *always* want to go shopping," Alicia said, laughing.

"Hey, it's my favorite hobby. And I'm already meeting a friend for lunch."

"A friend or a *friend*?" Grace asked.

"A *friend* named Carl," Paige replied with a mischievous smile.

"You go, girl!" said Grace, high-fiving her. "See you all tomorrow."

She waved good-bye, and Paige followed before Alicia had a chance to question her any more about her lunch date.

"What about you, Kalila?" asked Alicia.

"I'll have to ask my father first," she replied with a timid smile.

"Of course," said Alicia. "I understand. I have to get my father's permission to do *any*thing!"

Kalila glanced toward a sleek silver Mercedes-Benz in the parking lot. "Sorry, I'd better go—my brother's waiting for me."

Connor followed her gaze and spotted a young man in the driver's seat, looking in their direction and impatiently checking his watch.

"Bye, Connor, it's been lovely meeting you," said Kalila, smiling shyly at him before hurrying down the steps and over to the car.

"We should go too," said Alicia. "Otherwise Kyle will start getting edgy."

As Connor followed Alicia, he looked back at the silver Mercedes and remarked, "Kalila seems nice."

"Yes, she's one of my best friends. Her father's a foreign diplomat, so she's not fazed by the fact that I'm the first daughter."

"What do you mean?" asked Connor.

Alicia considered him a moment, then seemed to decide to trust him with her thoughts. "Having a father who's presi- dent can affect friendships. When my father was elected, some of my friends dropped away, worried they'd appear to be sucking up to me. Others, who'd never spoken to me before, tried to squeeze into my supposed 'inner circle.' But Kalila, she just stayed the same."

"It's good to have friends like that," said Connor, thinking of Charley and Amir back in the United Kingdom. He hoped he would get a chance to speak to them during his evening report.

As they headed down the school steps, Kyle subtly appeared from behind and guided them toward the waiting limo. He opened the door for Alicia. On the other side, another agent held the door for Connor.

"I trust you had a good first day, Connor?" asked Kyle as he shut Alicia's door.

"Tiring, but otherwise uneventful."

"That's *exactly* how it should be," he replied with a wink.

38

The two black limos turned down a side street just as a woman with a baby stroller walked out into the middle of the road. The driver of the lead limo put on his brakes, slowing to allow her to cross. But when the mother was halfway across, she reached into the stroller and drew out a large black gun. Aiming the muzzle at the limo's grille, she pulled the trigger.

Nothing happened *apparently*.

There was no bang. No sound of a bullet or projectile hitting the limo. Just a tiny mechanical *click* and a frisson in the air, like just before a bolt of lightning is about to strike.

The driver floored the accelerator. But the limo failed to respond.

Unseen by the human eye, an intense electromagnetic pulse had been unleashed. Channeling through the metalwork of each car, the massive energy surge fried all the internal circuitry. Both engines died. Power-assisted steering failed. So did the headlights, along with every other elec-tronic system that the handheld EMP weapon had knocked out—including radios and cell phones. In an instant, the two armor-plated limos were rendered useless hunks of metal. Without power or control, they simply hit the curb and jud-dered to a halt.

A second later, several armed men, their faces concealed by bandanas, broke from the cover of the side alleys. Keep-ing their weapons trained on the two immobile limos, they surrounded their targets and closed in.

Realizing they were sitting ducks, the agents jumped out of their vehicles to engage with the enemy. But snipers on the nearby roofs took each of them down before a single shot was fired in retaliation, their muffled long-range rifles sounding no louder than a whisper to ensure the ambush wasn't heard in the adjacent streets.

In fact, the entire attack was executed in sinister silence.

Inside the front limo, the remaining occupants were co-cooned within the armored box of the passenger section. No way in—but no way out for them either.

Kedar rushed forward and crouched beside the rear door. Pulling out a circular metal device from his backpack, he fixed it to the reinforced glass window.

"Keep clear!" he warned, sheltering behind the limo's bumper. Then he pressed a button.

A high-pitched whirring quickly built in intensity. Just

as the sound reached the limit of human hearing, the sonic charge shattered the bulletproof glass. Chunks, like cracked ice, fell to the ground. As soon as the security of the limo was breached, Kedar was at the window with his gun.

"Out!" he growled.

Malik's face appeared, a crooked smile on his lips. He checked his watch.

"Not bad, Kedar," he said. "The technology works. But your team needs to shave off another eight seconds."

He opened the limo door and looked around the disused industrial estate. The downed "agents" were getting to their feet, rubbing their chests where their bulletproof vests had taken the impact of the snipers' "simunition" rounds.

"Drill your men again," Malik ordered. "This ambush has *only* a sixty-second window of opportunity. I intend to seize it."

39

Connor collapsed on his bed in the White House guest room. His head aching, he closed his eyes for a moment while he waited for his laptop to boot up. Maybe it was jet lag or the strain of his first day on protection detail, or a combination of both, but he felt utterly drained. Colonel Black had insisted that Code Yellow became easier with practice. Connor seriously hoped that was the case; otherwise he'd likely burn out from exhaustion in the coming weeks.

He picked up his father's key fob from the bedside table. He'd overlaid the photo of himself with his father's, cut from the picture Colonel Black had given him. Squeezing the talisman in his hand, he wondered how his father could have done this job day in, day out. Although the training had been tough, Connor had never expected actual close protection to be so demanding—and nothing had really happened apart from going to school. But there was always an underlying pressure that came with the responsibility of protecting someone. He might have been the last ring in the Secret Service's defense, but if any attacker did get through, *he* would be the one held accountable for Alicia's life . . . or death. And that weighed heavily on his mind.

His laptop buzzed, and the Guardian logo flashed on the screen. Unlocking the device with his fingerprint, he clicked the Answer button. Charley's smiling face appeared. She looked fresh and vibrant, despite it being 1:00 a.m. in the United Kingdom.

"Caught you sleeping, did we?" she teased, seeing Connor rub the tiredness from his eyes.

"Almost," he admitted, yawning.

"Don't worry, your body will adjust to the time zone in a couple of days. When I was on assignment, it took me at least a week to get used to the new routine. How's your Principal?"

"Fine," replied Connor. "Alicia obviously dislikes having the Secret Service everywhere, but there's no sign of that impulsive streak you mentioned."

"Once she gets to know you, she may open up a bit more and show her true colors," said Charley.

Marc leaned into the camera's view.

"Is she as"—he raised his eyebrows meaningfully—"as she looks in the photos?"

Connor couldn't help smiling at Marc's off-assignment question. To tell the truth, he'd been concentrating so much on protecting his Principal that he hadn't considered that aspect since their first meeting. He couldn't deny that Alicia was very pretty. And in different circumstances he might have paid her looks a lot more attention. But that sort of thinking could become a dangerous distraction. Colonel Black had very clearly said that a guardian's role was to protect. Any involvement beyond friendship was a line *never* to be crossed when on assignment. It could cloud one's judgment and potentially endanger the protectee. Nonetheless, Connor grinned and nodded in reply to Marc.

"Well, don't get too cozy," said Charley sharply. "You're there to do a job. And, judging by the increased chatter on the Internet and our communications intercepts, your role is more vital than ever."

"Has a threat been made?" asked Connor, sitting up.

"Not directly. But there are indications of a number of terrorist attacks being planned against the United States. Nothing concrete, but the CIA and Secret Service are certainly twitchy. You should ask Dirk Moran for an update."

Connor gave a strained smile. "I'll ask, but he's not exactly welcoming me with open arms."

Charley nodded, immediately grasping the situation. "This often happens at the start of an operation. There's always someone who doubts the capability of a guardian. You'll have to gain the director's trust. Until then, that's what we're here for. I'll ask Amir to e-mail you an encrypted threat update."

"Thanks," said Connor. "At least I'll know what to watch out for."

"So, do you have anything to report?"

Connor shook his head. "Not really. It was a normal school day—or as normal as it can be for a guardian. At first I suspected everyone from students to teachers. But that can't last, so I'm going to study the staff list tonight. The drop-off and pickup by Secret Service is tight, as would be expected. Other than that, I learned how to say, 'Where's the bathroom?' in Chinese—*Cèsuǒ zài nǎli?*"

"*Hěn hǎo*," complimented Charley, yet again surprising Connor with her hidden talents. "Well, it's a good day when nothing happens. Let's hope it stays that way."

40

"Are you sure you want to join this class?" asked Alicia, raising a doubtful eyebrow at Connor. "You don't have to do *everything* I do, you know. Most of the boys have opted to play baseball."

"No, it's fine," said Connor. "I've always wanted to learn to dance properly."

Connor hoped he sounded convincing. He'd never considered dance class before in his life, but he needed to stay close by Alicia to do his job. As they entered the school gymnasium, Connor discovered, to his dismay, that he was one of only three boys in the entire class.

"Hey, over here!" called Grace, beckoning them to join her and Paige on a side bench. As they approached, Grace gave him an odd look. "I wouldn't have thought this was your sort of thing, Connor."

"You English boys are full of surprises," Paige said, giggling as she slipped on a pair of glittery dance shoes. "Have you done salsa before?"

"No," replied Connor, beginning to feel nervous at the prospect. "The closest I've ever gotten to salsa is some sauce with a bag of tortilla chips."

Despite the weakness of his joke, the girls all laughed. But they stifled their amusement when an elegant elderly lady appeared and clapped her hands for their attention. Connor recognized the woman from the staff photo file as Miss Ashworth, a former professional ballroom dancer who had toured the world several times.

"Class, we'll continue with the Cuban-style salsa step from the previous lesson," she announced, her tone clipped and precise. "Alicia and Oliver, would you please demonstrate?"

Alicia joined a young blond boy in front of the theater stage, and Miss Ashworth pressed Play on a CD player. A lively, percussion-filled, horn-heavy dance track filled the gym, and Oliver led Alicia through a series of seemingly complex moves. Connor watched in growing awe as they danced energetically to the music. Alicia was a natural mover, her hips swaying, her arms flowing and her feet shimmying across the floor in a dazzling, twirling display. Her ability was matched only by her enthusiasm. She literally threw herself into the music and seemed to come alive under its influence.

Miss Ashworth paused the CD. "Not bad," she conceded. "Just be careful where you put the break step. Now, everyone, find a partner."

Having seen what was expected, Connor stayed sitting where he was.

"That includes you, young man," said Miss Ashworth, noting his presence.

Connor smiled politely. "I'll just watch for the time being, if that's okay."

Miss Ashworth gave him a stern look. "No, it's *not* okay. If you're in my class, you dance. No exceptions."

Seeing Connor's trepidation, Alicia came over. "Don't worry, I'll partner with you."

"It's *you* who should be worried. I don't have much experience at this," he admitted, not wanting to embarrass Alicia—or himself.

"It's all right; I'll lead," she assured him.

"Well, on your feet, then!" he said, throwing caution to the wind.

They stood opposite each other in line with the other students. Alicia instructed him to take her right hand in his left and place his right hand on her upper back while she put hers on his shoulder.

"Now look at me," she said. "It's important that we stay in eye contact during the dance . . . and you need to come much closer."

Connor stared at her, feeling slightly awkward at being *so* close to his Principal.

"Don't look so nervous," she said, smiling. "It's just a dance."

To you it might be, thought Connor, wondering what Colonel Black would make of all this.

Miss Ashworth restarted the music, and the Latin American track once more filled the hall. Alicia instinctively found the beat and began moving to the rhythm. Connor attempted to follow Alicia's fluid steps, but quickly ended up looking like a malfunctioning puppet.

Alicia laughed good-naturedly. "No, like this," she said above the music, gently guiding him through the sequence. "You have to start on the third beat of the musical bar," she explained, clicking her fingers to the track. "One . . . two . . . Now break forward with your left foot. Good! Rock back on your right. Step back left. Now shift your weight to that foot. Step back right. Rock forward onto your left. Step forward right. Then shift your weight onto your right foot—and repeat. It's that simple."

"Simple!" exclaimed Connor, his mind whirling with the multiple directions as he stared down at his clumsy feet.

"No, look at *me*," encouraged Alicia. "Just let your body feel the music."

Connor continued to shuffle around, willing his mind and feet to function as one. But he couldn't quite get the two to meet. He stepped on Alicia's toes, and she cried out.

"Sorry," he said, moving away. "I think I must have two left feet."

"No, you haven't," chided Alicia kindly. "You just need a

bit more practice, that's all. Get the steps right, and then everything else will follow."

If only it were that easy, thought Connor, mentally repeating the moves over and over in his head.

As the other students whirled effortlessly around the gymnasium, Miss Ashworth noticed him struggling to master the steps and came over.

"Stay light on your feet," she instructed.

Connor was struck by her words. Dan, his kickboxing instructor, had often drilled the same phrase into him during training in the ring. Connor decided to switch his mind-set. And as soon as he began to think of the salsa moves as a martial arts *kata*, he quickly latched on to the combination and found the rhythm.

"That's more like it," said Alicia, stepping along with him to the music's groove.

At last they began to *really* dance, and Alicia's face lit up with delight. "See, I told you. You're actually not that bad."

Connor smiled at her praise and was beginning to get into the swing of things when his eye caught movement on the stage. The theater drapes were twitching. As he spun around with Alicia, he tried to focus on the gap in the curtains. There appeared to be someone peeking through . . . and Connor got the distinct feeling that he and Alicia were the ones being watched.

Suddenly Alicia switched direction in the dance. Distracted

by the suspicious observer, Connor mistimed his step, and his feet got mixed up with Alicia's. They both stumbled and went crashing to the floor, landing entangled in each other's arms. The whole class stopped and giggled in amusement. Miss Ashworth switched off the music.

"Are you two all right?" she asked.

"Yes," wheezed Alicia, "but only just!"

"I'm so sorry," said Connor, quickly getting up and helping her to her feet. "I hope I didn't hurt you."

"No, not at all," she replied, brushing herself down and now laughing at their fall. "But you should come with a health warning!"

"Young man, you need to concentrate more on what you're doing," scolded Miss Ashworth, turning back to the CD player. "Now, let's go from the top."

As the music struck up again, Connor snatched a glance toward the stage. The curtains were now still. The mysterious watcher—if there had been one—had gone.

41

The first week at Montarose School flew by. Following further advice from Charley, Connor had begun performing "dynamic" risk assessments—changing his level of alertness depending upon the situation. In class, he could allow himself to relax more, knowing they were in a controlled environment, overseen by a vetted teacher. During breaks and class changes, when the situation was more unpredictable, he heightened his awareness—staying in Alicia's vicinity and scanning for potential threats. By doing this, he could better manage his concentration levels and wasn't so exhausted by the end of a day.

In the evenings, he was allowed some downtime, since the White House was deemed a safe zone. Each night, after an hour of fitness and martial arts training in the gym, Connor delivered status updates to Guardian HQ. He called in even when there was nothing new to report, simply enjoying the chat with Charley and the chance to truly be himself. Afterward, he would check his e-mails, dutifully replying to his mother, who reassured him that all was well with her and Gran back in England.

By the end of the week, Connor had become accustomed to the routine and was actually enjoying his protective role. He liked Alicia and thought he was becoming her friend. There had been no real incidents, he'd made no apparent mistakes, and he began to wonder if the assignment was going to be easier than he'd first thought. With all the Secret Service protection in place, the greatest threat to Alicia at school so far was dying from boredom in a history lesson.

Having survived the Friday-morning period, Alicia and her friends headed over to the edge of the school playing field to sunbathe away the lunch break.

"You mean to say, you still haven't said yes!" gasped Paige.

"Ethan hasn't asked me properly . . . yet," replied Alicia.

Connor sat behind them on a picnic bench, pretending to read a book. From behind his sunglasses, he kept one eye on the open playing fields, conscious that Alicia was positioned in a highly exposed area.

"But we're only a week away from the dance," Paige reminded her.

"You should consider yourself lucky," said Grace. "No one's asked me yet."

"Or me," admitted Kalila.

"Boys our age are always shy about coming forward,"

said Paige, pushing herself up on her elbows. "Why is that, Connor?"

Connor glanced up from his book. "Sorry?" he replied, pretending not to have heard.

"Boys are scared to ask girls out. Why?"

Connor thought about his own experiences. "Probably because they think the girl will say no."

"He's got a point," agreed Grace. "There's only *one* boy I'd say yes to."

"Who's that?" Paige asked eagerly.

"Oh, come on, we all know she has a crush on Darryl," said Alicia.

"Is it *that* obvious?" cried Grace, mortified by the public declaration.

"I thought it was Jacob," said Kalila.

"That was last month," Alicia said, and laughed. She stood up and dusted the grass from her skirt as Paige began to interrogate Grace. "Back in a minute. I need to go to the bathroom."

"I'll join you," said Kalila.

Connor stayed where he was. There were *some* places he couldn't follow Alicia, and because they were on the school campus, he considered the increase in risk minimal. Still, as Alicia and Kalila strolled off together, he checked his watch and made a mental note of the time. Then he performed another subtle surveillance sweep of the playing field and surrounding buildings.

As the two girls entered the side entrance of the science wing, Connor noticed a man emerge from behind a tree and head toward the glass doors. He was wearing a green uniform and a baseball hat, its brim pulled low to shade his eyes . . . or possibly to hide his face.

Connor subconsciously raised his alert level from Code Yellow to Code Orange. "Who's that?" he asked, nodding in the man's direction.

Grace looked up from her phone and squinted. "Um . . . must be one of the groundskeepers. Why?"

The man followed Alicia and Kalila through the doors.

"Just wondering," Connor replied, alarm bells ringing inside his head. *What business does a groundskeeper have inside the science building?*

He excused himself and headed over to the science wing. Hurrying, but not quite running, he cursed himself for leaving so much distance between himself and his Principal. When he reached the doors, he quietly slipped inside. The corridor leading to the girls' restroom was deserted, apart from the suspect man, who was bent over near the restroom entrance.

He cautiously approached the man from behind. Connor wanted to get close enough to identify him, to find out whether he might be the same person as the one behind the kitchen door.

When Connor was a few feet away, the man looked up,

startled, water dripping from his stubbled chin. His face was grimy, rough and lined by the sun. He had a large bent nose, as if it had once been broken in a fight, and a pair of hound-dog eyes that were ringed with dark shadows, indicating a lack of sleep. *Was this the same face?* The eyes possessed a similar unsettling intensity. But Connor couldn't be certain. He did, however, vaguely recognize the man from the grounds-staff roster.

"Sorry, I know I shouldn't be here, but I needed a drink," the groundsman said in a thick accent. "Please don't report me. I've been digging all morning and was very thirsty."

Wiping his mouth with the back of his hand, he stepped away from the water fountain and quickly made his way out of the science building. Connor watched him go. He realized now that he'd probably overreacted to the man's behavior, but told himself it was better to be safe than sorry.

"Hanging around the girls' restroom?" sneered Ethan, approaching from behind. "Is that what English boys do for a hobby?"

Jimbo stood beside his friend, sniggering.

"Not every day," replied Connor. "Otherwise I'd always bump into you."

Ethan scowled at the comeback. "I've been watching you," he declared, stabbing a finger at Connor. "You follow Alicia around like some faithful puppy dog. Even attending her dance classes! What's going on between you two?"

"Nothing," said Connor, now realizing who the mysterious watcher might have been. "I'm just finding my feet, that's all."

"Well, find them somewhere else."

He pointed to a poster on the wall—a silhouette of a couple dancing against a glittery purple background that announced the forthcoming school dance. "*I'm* taking the president's daughter," he said, puffing out his chest, "and I don't want any dork getting in the way and spoiling my chances. Understand?"

Connor shrugged off the insult. Ethan might be the school's star athlete, but considering how arrogant he was, he didn't deserve to be Alicia's date.

"I said, do you understand?" repeated Ethan, taking a step closer. "Or do I have to get Jimbo here to beat it into you?"

Connor suddenly found himself boxed in on both sides. The two boys towered over him, the situation rapidly escalating toward a fight.

"Listen, I don't want any trouble," said Connor, holding up his hands in peace.

"Who said anything about trouble?" sneered Ethan as Jimbo closed in.

Deciding it was time for a touch of pain-assisted learning, Connor targeted the middle of the boy's chest with his fingertips.

"Ow!" cried Jimbo, stopping his advance.

Ethan glared at his friend. "What's the problem? You're an offensive guard in the football team. Steamroll him!"

Almost half his size, Connor judged that the massive American football player would flatten him if he didn't strike first. Snaking his arm with a hefty flick, Connor one-inch-pushed Jimbo in the chest. It was like trying to shove an elephant, but the self-defense technique was still powerful enough to send the boy staggering backward. Jimbo struck the wall behind him and crumpled against it, gasping for breath.

"What on *earth* did you do?" exclaimed Ethan, stunned by the ease with which Connor had downed his friend.

"I only pushed him," declared Connor innocently.

Ethan wound up to let loose a punch. Connor dropped into a fighting guard.

"Hey! What's going on?"

Ethan stopped midswing as Alicia and Kalila emerged from the bathroom. His scowl transformed into a beaming smile, and his punching arm wrapped around Connor in a friendly hug. "Just ... uh ... explaining to my friend here how to throw a Hail Mary pass," he replied.

Alicia gave them both a doubtful look. "What's the matter with Jimbo?"

"I think ... he's suffering from an asthma attack," replied Connor breezily.

"Well, aren't you going to help him up?" asked Kalila with concern.

"Of course," said Ethan. He patted Connor on the shoulder, rather too heartily. "Now bear in mind my advice for the school dance and you should have a great night," he said, before walking off with Jimbo in tow, the boy wheezing like a steam engine.

Connor doubted that very much. Having made enemies of them both, he knew the dance was going to be a nightmare. He'd already anticipated there'd be a tricky balance securing Alicia's safety while allowing her the freedom to enjoy herself. Now somehow he'd have to find a way to protect Alicia . . . without getting himself into a fight.

42

"This is the spot, on August twenty-eighth, 1963, where Dr. Martin Luther King Junior, the civil rights leader, delivered his famous 'I Have a Dream' speech," the tour guide explained to the group gathered on the steps of the Lincoln Memorial. Behind them stood the awe-inspiring monument itself, a white-marble cenotaph with towering Greek columns built in honor of America's sixteenth president. "The political march that day and Dr. King's speech helped facilitate the landmark Civil Rights Act of 1964, which outlawed discrimination throughout America."

Connor, Alicia and Kalila sat on the steps nearby, listening to the tour guide's talk.

Kalila leaned close to Alicia. "I bet Dr. King never dreamed that less than fifty years later, there'd have been an African-American president."

"Or a Latino one," replied Alicia, smiling at her friend.

"America's truly the land of the free. *Anyone* can be president— even my father!"

"Over a quarter of a million people attended the event," continued the tour guide, "with crowds stretching down the mall as far as the eye could see, thus making it, at that time, the largest gathering of protesters in the illustrious history of Washington, DC."

Connor gazed east across the impressive tree-lined expanse of the National Mall and tried to imagine such a number. There were no protests today, just flocks of tourists enjoying the sunshine beside the Reflecting Pool. In the distance, the Washington Monument speared the sky like a giant rocket ready to take off. The huge marble obelisk, the symbol of America's capital, shimmered in the pool's sky-blue waters and gave the illusion that the monument was twice its normal height.

"Wonderful, isn't it?" remarked Alicia.

Connor nodded in agreement, although in his mind he was actually thinking this was the *worst* possible place to be on a Saturday morning. Not because the view wasn't stunning but because Alicia was so vulnerable on the open steps. She was literally a sitting target. There was no cover if some madman took a potshot at her. No place to hide if she was attacked. Hundreds of tourists milled around and *any* one of them could be carrying a knife or a gun.

Connor almost wished he'd never done his bodyguard

training. It would be far easier to sit there in blissful ignorance of the countless hidden dangers surrounding them. At least then he could relax. But his assignment meant that he had to remain on constant alert, his nerves wound tight as a guitar string. Connor looked across at a slim blond-haired woman wearing sunglasses and carrying a pocket tourist guide. She too seemed to be enjoying the view. But every so often she'd glance in their direction.

But Connor wasn't alarmed. He recognized her as Agent Brooke, one of several women on Alicia's PES team. Other agents, including Kyle, were dotted around the Lincoln Memorial steps and along the edge of the Reflecting Pool, all within sight line of the president's daughter and each keeping a low profile so as not to draw attention to her presence. But Connor knew the strain the agents must be under, because he was feeling it too—the unpredictability of the situation, the uncertainty of the environment, the constantly changing dynamics of the crowd. No wonder the Secret Service had a hard time walking the thin line between the need for protection and their Principal's need for privacy.

"Let me take a picture of you," Alicia suggested to Connor. "This is *the* tourist spot."

"Why don't I take it?" offered Kalila. "Then you can both be in the photo."

"Good idea," said Alicia, jumping to her feet and waving Connor over.

Connor grinned. It would be pretty cool to have a photo of him with the president's daughter. At the very least, it would make Amir and Marc envious. Unlocking his phone's screen and clicking the camera app, he handed his phone to Kalila. Then he and Alicia posed on the steps of the Lincoln Memorial like every other tourist.

"Get closer, you two," said Kalila, lining up the shot.

As she took several photos from different angles, Connor began to notice a low buzz of excitement among the tour group. He glanced over and saw that several people were no longer listening to the guide. Instead they were staring in their direction. Or, to be more accurate, in Alicia's direction.

"Is it really *her*?" a large lady whispered to her equally bulbous husband.

"Looks like the president's daughter to me," he replied, holding up an image on his phone's web browser and comparing it with the dark-haired girl on the steps.

An Italian man, overhearing their conversation, plucked up the courage to take a sneaky photo of Alicia, while poorly feigning a shot of the Reflecting Pool behind. Connor instinctively began to shield Alicia from their attention.

"Shall we go?" suggested Connor as a Japanese man joined in, focusing his lens on the president's daughter's face with zero subtlety.

"What's the hurry?" Alicia replied, still looking toward

Kalila and oblivious to the rapidly growing interest. "You haven't seen Lincoln's statue yet."

"I can come back another day."

By now the tour group had all turned toward the president's daughter and were drawing nearer for a better shot. A tall man in a baseball hat and sunglasses was at Alicia's side in an instant.

"It's time to move on," said Kyle, his statement not quite an order, but leaving no room for argument either.

Alicia now saw the reason and smiled apologetically at the tour group. "Sorry, I've got to go!"

As word spread and the crowd began to thicken, Secret Service agents seemed to materialize out of nowhere. They drew into a "closed box" formation, creating a fluid cordon of protection around Alicia. Connor was by her side as the agents swiftly escorted her and Kalila down the steps and along the paved avenue toward the waiting limo. By the time they reached the car, the steps of the Lincoln Memorial were swarming with tourists, all attempting to catch a final glimpse of the president's daughter.

43

Secure within the confines of the limo, Alicia sat fuming on the backseat.

"Are you okay?" Kalila asked as the car and its escort vehicle pulled away from the gathered crowd.

Alicia didn't reply for a moment. She just stared through the darkened window at the passing traffic.

Then through clenched teeth, she said, "The Secret Service drives me crazy! I mean, those people were *only* taking photos."

"I'm sure Kyle had a good reason for asking us to leave," Connor said, glancing at the agent who sat on the other side of the glass privacy screen in the front passenger seat. He knew the Secret Service agents were used to dealing with crowds, so Kyle must have been alerted to another potential threat. In fact, he was *certain* something more than just a mob of tourists had spooked the agent.

"But I have to put up with this *all* the time!" Alicia cried, her frustration turning to anger. "At the slightest sign of . . . something . . . I don't know what . . . I'm whisked away. Usually, just as I'm starting to relax or—God forbid—enjoy myself. But how can I, when agents are always around me, dictating my movements, controlling my social life? Ironic, isn't it, Connor? I'm the first daughter in the land of the free, but I'm really a prisoner!"

"The Secret Service agents are there for your protection," Connor reminded her.

Alicia gave a weary sigh. "I know that, but why do they have to be so paranoid?"

"I suppose it's their job to be. So you—and your parents—don't have to worry about your safety."

"But they're robbing me of any life!"

"Isn't that a little extreme?" Kalila said gently.

Alicia shook her head furiously. "Not at all! Can you imagine spending every waking moment under surveillance? Seven days a week, twenty-four hours a day. I can't just walk out the door, meet up with my friends and go shopping. Everything has to be planned in advance. And forget about having a *boyfriend*. If I stay out later than my father approves, he orders the Secret Service to bring me home! And you try saying good night to a boyfriend at the door of the White House with the glare of floodlights and a

Secret Service agent by your side. There's not much you can do except shake hands. In fact, I'm amazed my father even let Connor stay in the White House!"

Connor offered Alicia an awkward smile, hoping she wouldn't press the matter any further. He'd worked hard not to expose his role as her personal bodyguard. But he needn't have worried; Alicia was too upset to read anything more into the situation. Her eyes began to glaze over with tears, and Kalila put a comforting arm around her friend.

"You think that's bad, then you clearly haven't met my brothers," she said, her voice gently soothing. "They're as overly protective as your Secret Service—and I have to put up with them for life!"

Alicia attempted a smile. "Sorry," she mumbled. "I didn't mean to get angry with you."

"I know," said Kalila, finding her a tissue from the seat's side pocket.

"It's just . . . so unbearable. Last month I wasn't allowed to leave the White House for a whole week because of some threat or other that came to nothing. And I missed out on Grace's sleepover."

"She understood. We all did."

Alicia took a deep breath. "But I feel like I'm *always* missing out."

"Then try not to let it ruin the rest of this weekend," said Kalila. "You've been given permission to be Connor's tour guide, and there's still a lot more of Washington to explore—the Capitol Building, the Washington Monument, the Air and Space Museum."

Alicia nodded and dried her tears. "Sorry, Connor. You must think I'm a spoiled princess."

"Of course not," he replied genuinely, having witnessed firsthand her claustrophobic life. "It must be tough having no privacy. But, at the same time, I can understand why you need Secret Service protection."

"But that doesn't make their presence any easier," she said, glancing bitterly toward Kyle, then gazing out the window at the pedestrians wandering freely about their business. "Sometimes I wish I could be someone else for a day—just disappear."

44

Connor stopped browsing the National Air and Space Museum's gift shop, suddenly aware that Alicia was no longer with him. "Where'd Alicia go?" he asked Kalila.

"She said she'll be back in a minute," replied Kalila, inspecting a soft toy monkey in a blue astronaut suit from the souvenir rack. "I can't believe NASA used monkeys to test the biological effects of space travel! That's so cruel."

Connor's eyes swept the gift shop as he absently picked up a cuddly bear in a white satin space suit and helmet. "Looks like they sent bears up too!" he joked, finally locating Alicia in the checkout line. He also spotted Kyle near the exit of the gift shop, pretending to be a father simply waiting for his family. Agent Brooke was posted at the entrance, another agent was at a door marked Private, and a fourth browsed the vast array of souvenirs like a typical tourist. With all exits covered, there was no way Alicia could just "disappear."

"Did you find any other souvenirs for your family?" asked Alicia, returning with a small foil bag in her hand.

Connor shook his head. He'd already bought a silk scarf for his gran and a Navajo feather bracelet for his mum from the American Indian museum. But with his assignment open-ended, he had no idea when he'd be able to give them the gifts personally.

Alicia handed him the bag. "I thought you might like to try this."

"Thanks," said Connor, examining the packaging. There was a picture of NASA's space shuttle taking off, with the words *Mission Pack: Freeze-Dried Ice Cream*. He looked at Alicia. "Are you serious?"

Alicia offered a wry smile. "Supposedly, the early Apollo astronauts ate it for a snack."

Ripping open the foil, he pulled out a multicolored block of Neapolitan "ice cream" that was bone dry and as light as Styrofoam. With trepidation, he bit off a chunk.

"Not bad. Tastes like . . . solid cotton candy," he said through a mouthful of the crumbling dehydrated dessert.

Since the incident at the Lincoln Memorial, Alicia and Kalila had taken him on a whistle-stop tour of the best sights along the National Mall. At the Museum of American History, he'd been shown the tattered red, white and blue flag that had inspired the US national anthem, "The Star-Spangled Banner." In the Museum of Natural History, he'd stood at the foot of a sixty-five-million-year-old Triceratops nicknamed Hatcher and gazed upon the 45-carat Hope Diamond once owned by Marie Antoinette—the jewel being surrounded by even more security than Alicia. Then, passing via the Museum of the American Indian, the three of them had finally ended up at the Air and Space Museum with its displays of spy planes, sound-barrier-breaking fighters and historic spaceships. To top it off, he'd had his photo taken in front of all the key landmarks, including the Washington Monument, the Capitol Building and even, for a joke, the White House.

Connor had been the ultimate tourist, and Alicia had tried her best to be his enthusiastic host. But the shadow cast by the ever-present Secret Service had dampened her spirits. Although she willingly joined him in the photos, her smile no longer quite reached her eyes.

"How about we go shopping?" suggested Kalila.

Although shopping wasn't high on Connor's list of favorite activities, the suggestion seemed to perk Alicia up.

"I suppose that's one benefit of the Secret Service," she said, managing a smile. "We always have a taxi on hand."

Leaving the Air and Space Museum, they jumped into the limo.

"Take us to Dupont Circle," said Alicia.

The driver nodded and headed northwest up Pennsylvania Avenue.

"But I thought you preferred the stores in Georgetown," said Kalila.

"I do, but I've heard there's a fantastic new boutique that opened up just off Connecticut Avenue," Alicia explained, and both girls began to get quite excited at the prospect.

Connor noticed Kyle talking rapidly into his wrist mic, no doubt instructing his advance team to scope out the intended clothing store before their arrival.

The SAP team didn't get long to do their sweep. The car ride only took ten minutes.

As the three of them entered the boutique, Connor recognized the watchful face of a Secret Service agent loitering near the entrance. As soon as Kyle's team had deployed themselves, he made a subtle exit with the rest of the SAP agents.

The store itself was a top-end boutique with wall-to-wall fashion from Europe, as well as unique garments from New York, LA and San Francisco. Alicia seemed to be in her element as she browsed the racks of designer clothes.

"What do you think of this?" asked Alicia, pulling out a sheer gold dress.

"It's gorgeous," gasped Kalila. "Are you thinking of wearing it to the school dance?"

Alicia nodded. "For you."

"No," she protested. "I couldn't get away with wearing that. Besides, I wouldn't be allowed to. It's far too short. But you could—" Kalila's phone beeped. She looked at the message and sighed. Texting a reply, she explained, "Sorry, I have to go home."

Alicia tried to hide her disappointment. "Do you want us to drop you off?"

"Thanks, but my brother's picking me up." Her phone beeped again. "Wow, he's parked just around the corner. I told you they're my own Secret Service!"

Alicia laughed, and the two girls hugged each other good-bye.

"See you on Monday, Connor," said Kalila.

Connor waved farewell as she hurried out of the store.

"Well, it looks like *you'll* have to be my clothes judge," declared Alicia, selecting a couple more glamorous dresses from the rack. "I'll just try these on, then we'll grab a bite to eat."

Connor watched Alicia make her way to the changing rooms and smiled to himself in bemused amazement. Never would he have imagined that one day he'd be shopping with the president's daughter, let alone giving advice on what she should wear.

"How's it going?" asked Kyle, appearing at Connor's shoulder.

"Fine," replied Connor. "But I think you're doing all the work."

Kyle shook his head. "There hasn't been one moment when

you weren't aware of your surroundings. Seems to me you're a natural at this game."

Connor smiled at the compliment—the first he'd received from the Secret Service. "What happened back at the Lincoln Memorial?"

"One of the team pinged a man on our threat list. Rather than cause a scene or alarm Alicia, I decided to simply avoid contact."

Alicia popped her head out of the changing-room cubicle and waved Connor over.

"Good luck!" Kyle remarked as he wandered off, to all intents and purposes appearing the bored husband waiting for his wife, rather than a Secret Service agent protecting the president's daughter.

Connor headed over to Alicia and stood beside her cubicle.

"Care to join me on a little adventure?" whispered Alicia, a mischievous grin on her face.

"What do you mean?" asked Connor.

Alicia glanced toward an emergency exit at the back of the store.

Immediately grasping her intentions, Connor replied, "I *don't* think that's a good idea."

"Oh, don't be such a killjoy! Even a soldier's son must have broken the rules."

"Your father wouldn't be happy."

"I don't *care* what he thinks," she shot back. "Besides,

what's the worst that could happen? I get recognized and asked for an autograph or photo."

Connor could imagine a whole host of other possibilities, none of them good.

"Anyway, if there's real danger, I have a panic alarm in my bag," Alicia insisted.

"I still think it's too risky," said Connor.

Alicia scowled. "Fine. Then don't come with me. I just thought it would be fun."

She beckoned the shop assistant over. "I think that lady over there might be a shoplifter," she whispered, pointing to a blond-haired woman browsing a nearby rack. "I'm sure I saw her put something in her bag."

"Thank you, I'll call security," replied the assistant, taking Alicia at her word.

Connor looked over his shoulder at the shoplifter, only to discover that the accused was Agent Brooke. A few moments later, a burly security guard approached her and asked to inspect her bag. While the agent was distracted, Alicia bolted for the emergency exit.

Connor realized he had to alert Kyle. It was his duty. But if he did tell Kyle, Alicia would know and she'd no longer confide in him as a friend. He'd lose that essential connection that enabled him to be an effective and covert bodyguard.

Caught between a rock and a hard place, Connor had no choice but to follow her.

45

Bursting out the back door into an alley, Alicia was off like a shot. Connor was on her tail, but he was left in the dust as she sprinted past some Dumpsters and disappeared around a corner.

"Wait!" cried Connor, realizing now why Alicia was the captain of her school track team.

He pursued her down a deserted side street. But Alicia was still pulling away.

"Keep up!" she called, giggling at the thrill of her escape.

Grateful for all his fitness training, Connor put on a burst of speed. His sneakers pounded the concrete as he followed her left onto the main road. Then he lost her . . .

The sidewalk was crowded with shoppers, and there was no sign of Alicia. Connor threw his hands up in despair. He was her sole bodyguard now, and he'd lost track of her within the first minute. Just as he was about to shout her name, a hand grabbed him from behind and pulled him into a shop doorway.

"Careful, they might spot you!" Alicia whispered, her eyes full of rebellious delight.

Connor realized Charley had been right. Only now was Alicia showing her true colors. And the president's daughter had never looked happier. Like a bird freed from its cage, she was all aflutter with excitement.

Alicia snatched a quick peek up and down the street.

"Not a Secret Service agent in sight!" she said, laughing.

And she thinks that's good news, thought Connor. The real pressure of protection was now on his shoulders—and his alone.

Oblivious to Connor's worries, Alicia opened her bag and pulled out a short platinum-blond wig and a large pair of dark sunglasses. Pinning up her hair, she popped on the wig, then slipped on the Jackie Onassis–style glasses. In an instant she was transformed from president's daughter to . . . anybody.

"How do I look?" Alicia asked.

"You planned this!" Connor exclaimed.

"Yes," she admitted with a half-guilty smile. "President Johnson's daughter used to wear a disguise to dodge the media. I thought I could do the same to escape the Secret Service."

Connor was astonished at the lengths Alicia was willing to go to for some personal space.

"Come on, let's go," said Alicia, joining the stream of pedestrians.

"Where to?" asked Connor.

"U Street. It has some cool places to shop and eat."

Connor stayed close by Alicia's side. If anything did happen, he wanted to be within arm's reach and able to react fast. From behind his mirrored sunglasses, he scanned their surroundings just as Bugsy his surveillance instructor had taught him. His eyes flicked between the faces of approaching people, making snap decisions about their intentions. He watched the passing traffic for any suspicious vehicles, while noting any nearby alleyways in case someone was concealed there. In the highest state of Code Yellow, he had to be alert to *anything* that could materialize into a threat. The good thing was that Alicia was no longer identifiable as the president's daughter. That reduced the risks, but didn't eliminate them entirely. Every city had its fair share of crime, violence and accidents—and Washington, DC, was no exception.

Alicia's cell phone rang. She glanced at the screen, tutted, then turned it off.

A second later, Connor's phone rang too. Pulling it from his jeans pocket, he saw caller ID withheld but knew exactly who it would be—Kyle. As his thumb hovered over the Answer button, Alicia snatched the phone from his grasp.

"Give that back!" said Connor.

"Later," she said, offering him a playful wink.

Connor made a grab for the phone, but she danced away. "I should at least reply, so they know we're okay."

"What are you so worried about? Let them sweat a bit."

Alicia switched off his phone before dropping it into her bag. Then she trotted off down the street.

Connor sighed in frustration. He didn't want to make a scene. That could draw unwanted attention to the president's daughter, so he resigned himself to letting her have her own way—for the time being.

Quickening his pace, he caught up with Alicia. Every so often he glanced behind them, checking for trouble but also secretly hoping to spot an agent in pursuit.

"Relax," insisted Alicia, taking his arm. "Just let me enjoy myself for once. I'm the one who'll get into trouble later."

That's what you think, mused Connor. Then it dawned on him that this was exactly what he'd been hired for. To protect Alicia in moments when the Secret Service couldn't. Colonel Black had specifically instructed him "to stick to her like glue." He wasn't supposed to keep Alicia from living her life—just protect her.

With that thought in mind, he allowed himself to relax a little. But he kept his awareness at Code Yellow.

They turned off the main street and headed north on Thirteenth. Upscale apartments gave way to run-down row-house blocks, which alternated randomly with fancy condos recently built as part of the city's redevelopment effort. The strange blend of new and old, rich and poor made Connor uneasy. The mix of people walking the streets became more diverse and unpredictable. There was a palpable tension in the air, magnified by the summer's heat radiating off the sidewalk.

"Are you certain this area's safe?" Connor asked.

"Of course," replied Alicia, casually strolling along. "During the day, definitely."

That statement didn't reassure Connor. Although he could handle himself in a situation, there were places in the East End of London that he wouldn't wander into—day or night. And this area possessed a similar undercurrent of menace.

46

The phone emitted a short buzz, and Bahir snatched it up from the table in the front room. He waited an impatient second for the message to decrypt. Then his eyes widened in astonishment.

"You won't believe this, Malik," he said, holding up the phone to his leader. "Eagle Chick has flown the nest!"

Malik stopped sharpening his *jambiya* and smirked to himself. "It's almost as if she *wants* to be taken hostage."

The phone buzzed again, and Bahir read the message out loud. "It's from Hazim—*Sparrows in a panic*. It appears the Secret Service agents are having trouble locating her!" He laughed. Bahir turned excitedly to his leader. "*This* could be our chance."

Malik laid the curved dagger in his lap. His right hand trembled slightly, and he reached out to a small bundle of khat. As he chewed the leaves, he mulled over the new turn of events.

"Yes, it's an opening," he agreed. "But an unplanned one. Not all the preparations are in place."

"But this seems too good an opportunity to miss," insisted Bahir.

"The situation isn't in my *direct* control," pointed out Malik. "And we have the added complication that the Secret Service agents are *actively* looking for her at this time. That greatly reduces our chances of an undetected escape."

"True, but if we took her now, alone, we wouldn't risk our lives in a gun battle."

Malik pondered his words. "Do either Gamekeeper or Birdspotter have the target in sight?"

Bahir rapidly typed a message and pressed Send. Almost a minute passed before his cell phone vibrated twice in response. He read both messages, then grimaced in disappointment. "Not yet, but Gamekeeper and Birdspotter are on the hunt."

Malik rested the tip of his knife on his bearded chin, reconsidering his options. Then a sly grin slid across his face, revealing his arc of yellowing teeth. "Bahir, I have an idea."

He explained his plan, then asked, "Is such a thing possible?"

"Yes," replied Bahir. "I could do it in my sleep."

"Then get to it," ordered Malik.

As Bahir hurried out of the room, Malik returned to honing his *jambiya*, the curved steel blade turning razor sharp.

47

With every step, Connor was becoming more and more anxious. He was about to suggest that they turn back, when Alicia swung right onto U Street and the neighborhood suddenly improved. Restaurants, bars, music clubs and the occasional church lined the busy road. Connor was reassured when he spotted several groups of tourists wandering the route too, but he didn't allow his alert level to drop.

Alicia stopped outside a red-and-white building with a neon sign flashing Open in the window. Above the door, a billboard proclaimed:

DON'S DOGS—
THE BEST CHILI DOGS IN DC

Connor noticed Alicia staring intently at the flashing sign as if mesmerized.

"Are you all right?" he asked, recalling her history of epilepsy from his Guardian briefing.

Alicia blinked and refocused her gaze on Connor. "Yes, of course. Why?"

"I thought . . . you might be about to have a seizure," he replied, nodding toward the flashing light.

"How do *you* know about my epilepsy?" demanded Alicia, suddenly defensive.

Connor realized he'd made a mistake. "Um . . . your father mentioned it."

Alicia scowled at this. "I'm *over* that now. I wish he'd stop bringing it up."

"Sorry," said Connor. "He's probably just concerned, that's all."

"My father's always worrying about me," sighed Alicia. "Anyway, this is the place I was looking for. Supposedly, their hot dogs are seriously *hot*."

Connor peered in through the smeared window. A white Formica counter stretched the short length of the fast-food joint. On the wall behind, a menu displayed its combo meals and specialties in unappealing backlit photos. Red plastic stools stood in contrast to the off-white tiled floor, some of the seats clearly straining under the weight of their well-fed customers. Opposite the counter were four booths, with only one occupied by two large men in grime-stained construction clothes.

The food better be good to make up for the decor, thought Connor.

As he held the door open for Alicia, a waft of fried meat and cooking fat assaulted Connor's nostrils. Behind the counter and through a hatch, a sweaty cook served up piles of cheese fries and massive hot dogs slathered in mustard, chili sauce and onions. He gave a nod in their direction, indicating with a grunt for them to take a booth. Slipping into the second one, Connor made sure that he sat facing the entrance. As dictated by his training, he wanted to know exactly who was coming and going.

While Alicia studied the menu—which unsurprisingly consisted of various combinations of hot dog—he took the opportunity to check out the restaurant. It was crucial to locate any exit points in case of trouble. Looking over his shoulder, he spotted a door leading to a communal restroom, which he guessed would likely be a dead end. Through a hatch behind the counter, he saw a red emergency exit sign pointing to the back of the kitchen. If anything did happen, Connor decided that would be the route he'd take with Alicia.

"What are you going to have?" asked Alicia as the waitress came over.

"Um . . . whatever you're having," he replied, not even looking at the menu.

"Two chili dog specials with large Cokes," said Alicia.

With a tired smile, the waitress took their order, then went back to the hatch and handed it to the cook.

Connor glanced along the counter. An old man in a brown polo shirt sat eating a hot dog. Next to him a young man in ripped jeans and a white T-shirt was picking at a tray of fries. As he dipped several in the ketchup, he casually eyed Alicia's Prada handbag lying on their table. Connor realized that, although Alicia might be able to disguise who she was, she couldn't disguise her wealth or social status.

Leaning forward, Connor whispered to Alicia, "I'd keep your bag beside you."

She took his advice without protest. And Connor relaxed a little when the young man directed his attention back to his food. The waitress returned and dumped two hot dogs drowning in mustard and chili, along with a pile of cheese fries and two bucket-sized Cokes. Connor was slightly taken aback at the size of the hot dog—it was well over a foot long.

"Enjoy!" said the waitress, almost as if it was a command rather than a wish.

The two of them started eating. After just one bite, Connor had to admit that it was the best hot dog he'd ever tasted . . . Then the roof of his mouth was almost blown off by the heat of the chili.

Alicia laughed as she saw tears streaming down his face. "I warned you they were hot!"

Spluttering, Connor grabbed his Coke and chugged down several mouthfuls.

Once he'd recovered enough to speak again, Alicia began to quiz him on his life back in England—where he lived, which school he went to, his parents, which countries he'd been to, whether he'd met the queen and so forth. Connor gave his answers as truthfully as possible without revealing his double role. He didn't like deceiving Alicia—it wasn't in his nature—but he understood why it was necessary.

Finishing off their meal, they both leaned back in the booth and gave a contented sigh.

"That was an awesome hot dog," said Connor. "Even with the chili."

Alicia nodded in agreement and wiped her lips with a napkin. "And do you know what's even better?"

Connor shrugged.

Alicia lowered her voice. "This is the first meal I've had outside the White House with no one looking over my shoulder."

At that moment, the door opened and two young Latino men entered. Dressed in baggy jeans and white sneakers, they had tattoos up their arms and red bandanas around their heads. One of them, boasting a gold front tooth, stared hard in Connor's direction. Connor immediately averted his gaze. He didn't want to antagonize them in any way. But as they took two stools at the counter, Connor kept them in his line of sight. The other guy, sporting a crew cut, eyed up Alicia with an appreciative sneer before turning to place his order.

Troubled by their presence, Connor suggested to Alicia, "Let's make a move."

"You mean go back?"

"It might be a good idea. Kyle and the others must be going crazy by now."

Alicia groaned. "Not yet. I'm enjoying myself too much. Let's go up to Meridian Hill Park. It has a great view of DC, and every weekend there's a drumming circle."

She waved to the waitress for the bill. Connor reached for his wallet.

"No, I'll pay," Alicia insisted, pulling a Platinum American Express card from her purse.

The waitress raised an eyebrow in surprise. "No cards," she said, thumbing toward a scrappy sign above the register that said Cash Only.

Alicia sifted through her purse and pulled out a hundred-dollar bill.

"Don't you have anything *smaller*?" asked the waitress.

Alicia shook her head. "Sorry."

With poorly concealed irritation, the waitress took the money. While they waited for their change, the two tough-looking guys at the counter sipped on their Cokes but didn't order any food. Connor's sense of unease grew.

The waitress returned and managed her first genuine smile when Alicia left a hefty tip.

"Come back soon," she called.

Unlikely, thought Connor as they stepped onto U Street.

Turning right, Alicia headed north again on Thirteenth. But they'd only gone one block when Connor had the distinct feeling they were being followed. Pretending to watch a car pass by, his eyes swept the road and sidewalk. Among the scattering of pedestrians, he instantly recognized the guy with the gold tooth walking several paces behind them, nonchalantly slurping on his Coke. Connor told himself it could be pure coincidence. The man probably lived nearby. But, to leave no doubt, Connor decided to employ some anti-surveillance techniques.

"Let's cross the road," he suggested to Alicia. "Stay out of the sun."

"Sure," said Alicia.

At the next junction, they switched to the other side. Connor snatched a look over his shoulder.

Gold Tooth had crossed the road too. Connor felt his heart rate increase. "Mirroring" was one of the key signs. But this could still be an innocent matter of circumstance.

"Hold on, Alicia, my shoelace is untied," said Connor, bending down.

As he pretended to retie his lace, he glanced behind. Gold Tooth had also stopped, appearing suspicious as he hung around a parked car. But then he finished his Coke and dumped it in a trash can.

"Not far now," said Alicia, oblivious to their tail. "It's left here. Then just two blocks down on the right."

They stopped at a crosswalk on the junction of Thirteenth and W Streets. For Connor, this was the moment of truth. If Gold Tooth followed them toward the park, he knew they were in serious trouble.

48

"I really appreciate you doing this," Kalila said to her brother as they drove in ever-widening circles around the clothing store.

"No problem," he replied.

"I just can't believe she actually ran off. Alicia always *threatens* to do so, but I thought she was joking."

"Don't worry, we'll find her."

"But Kyle was really panicking," said Kalila, recalling the strained look on the agent's face as he'd come sprinting out of the boutique and over to their car. Kyle had clearly hoped that as her friend she'd know where Alicia was or at least what she'd been planning. But Alicia's disappearance was as much a mystery and surprise to her as it was to the agent.

Kalila took out her phone and tried dialing Alicia for a third time.

Her brother glanced at the cracked screen. "I need to get you a new phone," he said.

"Oh, it's all right," she replied, putting the phone to her ear. "This one works fine . . . *Alicia?*" Kalila let out a sigh and lowered the phone to her lap.

"Any luck?" asked her brother.

"No, just goes to voice mail," she replied, and resumed her search out the window. "I hope she's okay."

Kalila's gaze swept over the stream of pedestrians as they cruised along W Street. Her eyes flicked from face to face, praying she'd spot her friend. But it was like looking for a needle in a haystack. Then just as they passed through the crossroads on Thirteenth Street, Kalila caught a glimpse of someone she recognized.

"Hey, that's Alicia!" she cried, her head whipping around to get another look.

"Are you sure?" said her brother, applying the brakes hard.

A car honked behind in annoyance.

Kalila nodded. "She's wearing a blond wig and sunglasses, but I'd recognize her Prada bag anywhere. It's limited edition. Besides, I saw her friend Connor too."

Another angry blast of car horns.

Her brother slapped the steering wheel in frustration. "It's a one-way street," he muttered, driving on. "We'll have to loop back at the next junction."

"Shouldn't we call Kyle?" said Kalila. "You have his card."

"Let's pick Alicia up first," her brother replied with a smile. "Just so we make sure it's her."

As a red light forced him to wait at the next junction, Hazim slipped out his phone and secretly texted his uncle:

Eagle Chick located. Junction 13th and W Street.

In disguise. Blond wig & sunglasses.

Need to swoop fast.

49

The seconds counted down with excruciating slowness as Connor waited with Alicia for the pedestrian signal to turn green. A few yards behind, Gold Tooth loitered on the corner, jabbering into his phone. Connor's alert level had rocketed to Code Orange, and he was ready to react at the slightest threatening move from the gang member.

The signal turned from red to green, and Connor followed Alicia across the road, ensuring he was between her and Gold Tooth at all times. On the far side they bore left and made for the park. There were no pedestrians on the sidewalk ahead, so Connor risked a glance back. Gold Tooth still had his ear clamped to his phone and was walking on past the junction.

"Have you listened to anything I've just said?" asked Alicia.

"Sorry," said Connor, allowing his awareness to return to Code Yellow.

"The Meridian Hill Park is nicknamed Malcolm X Park. It has a thirteen-step waterfall—"

Alicia came to a sudden halt as a young guy stepped out from behind a van and blocked their path. Connor cursed himself for letting his guard down. He'd been so focused on Gold Tooth, he'd forgotten about the one with the crew cut. Crew Cut was a good foot taller than Connor, and his arms boasted not only tattoos, but vicious scars from numerous knife fights. These guys had all the marks of being in a gang.

In the second that followed, Connor instinctively applied the A-C-E procedure from his training.

Assess the threat: gang member, high probability of carrying a knife or gun, 100 percent certainty of an attack.

Counter the danger: priority one—provide body cover for the Principal, then . . .

Escape the kill zone: evacuation options— (A) fight way through the threat but risk injury; (B) turn around and retreat but danger of exposing back to knife or gun attack; (C) take side street to next busy road and find safety in numbers.

Grabbing Alicia by the shoulder, Connor took option C and pulled her toward the side street.

"RUN!" he shouted, keeping himself between her and the gangster.

Alicia was too stunned to do anything but obey. Yet no sooner had they begun to flee than Gold Tooth jumped out from a nearby alley and cut off their escape route.

"Where *you* going so fast!" he said, grinning to reveal his gleaming tooth.

Connor spun to take Alicia back the way they'd come. But Crew Cut was bearing down on them from behind.

"Yo, girl, give us the bag," Gold Tooth demanded.

Connor looked around. There were no other people in sight to call for help, the two gang members having picked their mugging spot carefully. Panicking, Alicia became frozen to the spot, and Connor recognized the symptoms of "brain fade." He, on the other hand, was already pumped with adrenaline and able to think straight.

"Do as he says," urged Connor, hoping that would put an end to their predicament. It was far better to lose a fancy bag than an invaluable life.

Alicia moved as if to comply, but as she unshouldered the bag, her hand dived in. Gold Tooth grabbed the Prada bag and wrenched it from her grip.

"No tricks, girl," he spat. "You ain't using no Mace spray on me. That'll cost you your necklace."

"No," Alicia protested, her hand going protectively to the silver chain. "It was my grandmother's."

"Well, it's mine now."

Gold Tooth snatched for his prize. Connor instinctively stepped in to protect Alicia. But Gold Tooth got his fingers around the chain. Alicia jumped back, her wig and glasses dislodging as she fought to free herself. Her long dark locks tumbled out, and Gold Tooth, taken by surprise, let go.

"What the—?" he yelled. Then his eyes widened in recognition. "I know you—"

Seizing on the distraction, Connor made his move. The situation demanded an all-or-nothing approach, and he drove the edge of his hand into Gold Tooth's throat. The sudden attack cut off the gangster's air supply. Gold Tooth's eyes bulged as he fought to breathe. He dropped Alicia's bag, and its contents spilled across the sidewalk.

Connor immediately followed up with a hook punch to the solar plexus, then a lightning-fast uppercut to the jaw. There was a bone-jarring crunch, and the gangster's gold tooth flew from his mouth. It was over in less than five seconds: the final punch knocked the former Gold Tooth unconscious, and he collapsed to the sidewalk in a heap.

Alicia dropped to her knees, scrabbling for the contents of her bag.

"Leave it," said Connor, his priority her escape.

"Behind you!" cried Alicia as Crew Cut now charged in.

Connor spun to face the other gang member. In Crew Cut's hand flashed the ominous steel glint of a switchblade. Alicia screamed as she saw the knife plunge into Connor's side.

To be continued . . .

The Next Pulse-Pounding Adventure Is Available in Bookstores Now!

Turn the Page for a Sneak Peek at

Book 2: Hostage

Hazim sat on the edge of his bed, the Glock 17 cradled in his lap.

The handgun was light, less than two pounds fully-loaded. But the weapon weighed heavy on his conscience.

He recalled how the soldiers had fallen under the storm of bullets from the submachine gunfire at the shooting range. How the target of a woman had spun and juddered as he'd winged her with a couple of shots. How a red haze had descended over him. Then how he'd literally *shredded* the little girl with the teddy bear in her arms before managing to release the trigger.

At the time it had all seemed like a harmless carnival game, with no real casualties. But now the truth confronted him in all its hard simple clarity, the reality as blunt as the bullets he'd just loaded into the gun.

It wouldn't be cardboard targets that were hit with these lethal rounds.

It would be flesh and blood.

People would die.

Children.

How could God condone such acts?

Whether an infidel or not, they were all human. Didn't the holy text say that the slaying of one human life was the same as slaying all mankind?

Yet his uncle had argued that non-believers were *not* the same. That disbelief was worse than killing and therefore the killing of non-believers justified. So infidels didn't warrant the same holy protection as those of the Faith.

And when it came to testing his own faith, could he kill in the name of God?

Hazim knew his faith was strong. But was it strong enough for the struggle ahead?

The  Missions

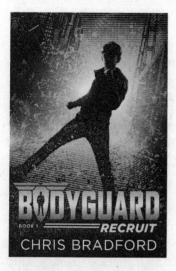

ACKNOWLEDGMENTS

The journey of a book from idea to completion is fraught with many dangers: from deciding the plotline, to creating believable characters, to actually writing the book, to defeating the self-doubt which plagues all authors! The dangers only increase when the book is launched in a new territory. Fortunately I had an expert team of "bodyguards" to protect me in my mission to publish the Bodyguard series in the United States. The fearless protectors who deserve my thanks are:

Brian Geffen, my editor at Philomel Books, whose enthusiasm and passion for the books is without bounds. Thank you for making the editing process so easy and enjoyable.

Michael Green, Publisher, whose unique approach to stimulating a "binge-reading" concept for the series is inspired! Thank for taking the "risk" on Bodyguard.

Laurel Robinson, my copy editor, one of the unsung heroes in process of crafting a book so it's the very best it can be.

Back in the UK, a huge thanks goes to Tig Wallace, my ever-loyal bodyguard of a first editor, and Camilla Borthwick for her flag waving of the series.

I also wish to acknowledge my darling wife, Sarah, my super-charged Zach and my glorious Leo; my mum and dad who have protected me my entire life; Sue and Simon for their love and support; guardians Steve and Sam; and Karen, Rob and Thomas of "Rose Security Forces."

Charlie Viney, my agent, who I believe would actually throw himself in the line of fire to protect my career!

My friends who continue to stand by me in life, including but not exclusive to Geoff and Lucy, Matt, Charlie, Nick and Zelia, Ann and Andrew (my godparents), my cousin Laura and the Dyson clan (especially my god-daughter Lulu!).

A huge thanks must go to the friends I made on my close-protection course. These people are real bodyguards and deserve true respect. This book is written in honor of them: Mandie, Simon, George, Sarah and Andy, Big Si, Baz, Andy, Jimmy, Sean, Nigel, Alex, Joe, Ronnie and of course Sam and Mark!

To my instructors on the Wilplan Close Protection Course (www.wilplantraining.co.uk) where I learnt the true art of being a bodyguard. Gary, Simon, Claire, Wendy, John, Ray and Pete—thank you for your dedicated instruction, patience and knowledge. Your wisdom is the lifeblood in this book.

And finally to you, my readers—read, enjoy and stay safe!
— Chris

Any fans can keep in touch with me via my YouTube channel ChrisBradfordAuthor or the website www.chrisbradford.co.uk